Suburban Gangsters

by Michael P. Dineen

DORRANCE
PUBLISHING CO
EST. 1920
PITTSBURGH, PENNSYLVANIA 15238

Dorrance Publishing Co
585 Alpha Drive
Pittsburgh, PA 15238
Visit our website at www.dorrancebookstore.com

ISBN: 978-1-4809-5189-1
eISBN: 978-1-4809-5167-9

Acknowledgements

I would like to thank my parents, Big Mike and Eileen, and my sister Colleen for never giving up on me. A thank you to my daughter Samantha for believing in me. Thank you to Christine T. for bringing me through the fire. And a very special thanks to Journee Wyatt, "You are the light at the end of my tunnel!"

This book is dedicated to anyone whose life has been touched by either drugs or crime. This is one crazy world we live in.

Prologue

A wise man who goes by the name of Jay-Z was once quoted saying, "Don't knock the hustle." For those of you who need to be enlightened, he is talking about a person who is being critical or overly judgmental toward someone who was caught up in the hustle game trying to make a living. The hustle could have represented a lot of different things. For my boys and me in New York, it meant either the drug trade or robbery. Now drugs have been around for thousands of years. Marijuana's use can be traced back as far as the third millennium BCE. Almost every type of people has used it consistently throughout history for many different reasons. The most common uses are for the psychedelic high it brings the user. Here in the United States, its use has skyrocketed due to the fact that it is now legal in many states.

The use of opiates can be dated back almost as far as 6,000 years ago as ancient Babylonians drank the sap and made cakes from the opium poppy (*Papaver Somniferum*) to kill pain and enhance the pleasures of sex. It was known as the joy plant or flower of joy. Alexander the Great and the ancient Greeks and Romans all used opium for a multitude of reasons. Roman Emperor Marcus Aurelius is widely considered history's first well-known opium addict. As useful as it was, there was a major downside to its usage, which was addiction. By 150 AD, the physician Galen warned people about the dangers of being physically bound to the drug. This drug was so powerful that centuries later, it caused actual wars between Great Britain and China in the 19th century. And it was during that century that other, more powerful forms of the drug would be synthesized. Morphine, which was first discovered in 1804, was looked at as a miracle drug. Its primary use is as a painkiller but was also used to treat alcohol addiction and respiratory ailments. Between morphine and the invention of the hypodermic needle in 1857, it would have its most purposeful use during the Civil War. Soldiers would be able to endure excruciating wounds and operations that were nearly impossible to cope with before. The Civil War would cause almost half a million men to become addicted to morphine and opium. As bad as this was, it would only get worse. A new drug, heroin, which was introduced by the Bayer Company, would hit the market in 1898. Thought to be a cure for morphine addiction, it was actually ten times stronger and much more addictive. It would cause the first major drug epidemic in this country. By 1900, there were an estimated 200,000 to 1,000,000 people hooked on heroin or its derivatives in the USA. At that time, you could buy it right over the counter in drug stores. This escalating problem would set in motion the creation of some of the first drug laws nationwide. The Harrison Act of 1914 would ban its sale and illegal use. This would ultimately lead to the opening up of the first black market trading of heroin and other narcotics. The mafia was really the first to get their hands into the cookie jar, and their involvement in heroin distribution dates back as early as the 1920s.

Salvatore Charles "Lucky" Luciano would go on to create one of the most elaborate and sophisticated heroin pipelines of all time starting around 1930. Lucky Luciano and Jewish gangster Meyer Lansky saw the potential in profits in heroin as unlimited, and also as a great way to keep the prostitutes of the more than 200 brothels in line. Heroin's popularity and use would start to fade, thanks in part to World War II and the federal efforts to do away with organized crime. For a short time, heroin's use declined greatly and would hit an all-time low. After Luciano's arrest, conviction, and then release from prison following World War II, he would rebuild his heroin empire. It would roll like a well-oiled machine for many years. By the 1970s, big busts such as the French Connection and the Pizza Connection in the 1980s would start to dismantle the mafia's involvement in the heroin trade. By then, other ethnic gangs and criminal organizations would be well on their way to establishing a foothold in the business. Chinese triads and some high-ranking figures in New York's Chinatown would be the next in line to flood the market with their "China White." China White is heroin manufactured in Southeast Asia with a purity rate of 96 percent. Overdoses and deaths would reach ridiculous levels to the 1980s onward. The morgues in New York City were overflowing with victims of this newer more potent smack. In February of 1989, the feds busted a 900 pound load of pure Southeast Asian heroin in a truck in Queens, New York. This shows you the numbers that were in play here. And then there would be more. Afghanis, Mexicans, and Columbians would all eventually enter this lucrative market, trying to take over their own piece of it with their own brand of the drug.

Cocaine is the other major drug in this story. Its class is considered as a local anesthetic, but it is also a stimulant. For over 1,000 years, South American indigenous people have chewed the leaves of the coca plant for energy and strength. From these leaves cocaine is produced. It was 1855 when the first cocaine alkaloid was isolated. It was an instant hit when it hit the market. Cocaine was used for many things from toothaches to morphine addiction. Sigmund Freud was one of its earliest users, and he loved it. By 1885, it was an ingredient in the soft drink Coca-Cola and would not be removed from the product until 1929. Cocaine would be a drug of choice until around 1914 when the Harrison Act again would make it much harder to obtain. For certain reasons, it became hardly available for decades until its resurgence in the 1970s. Now this time its usage would explode to an all-time high. The liberal attitude toward drugs following the 1960s would set the stage for what would eventually become nothing short of a national disaster. No one could have imagined what was to come. The cocaine trade was now being controlled by well-organized Colombian cartels that would open the floodgates for the modern hustle or dope game. This situation would spawn a new generation of gangsters and hustlers that law enforcement was completely unprepared for. By the early 1980s, it was everywhere. Everybody was doing it, and countless people were selling it. Crime would reach all-time highs in New York City and Long Island. You would have to have seen what was going on to believe it. And it wasn't just regular people committing crime. Police corruption would soar to unimaginable heights. This is around the time where this becomes my story and the crew I was involved with. We started out as not so ordinary kids, but would go on to become some of this country's worst "Suburban Gangsters."

Part I

Climbing the Ladder

My name is Patrick Hunter, and I grew up in the scenic little town of Huntington, Long Island in New York. Huntington was a sprawling suburban community with old-fashioned values and a new generation of kids who were going to turn this place upside-down. I was born in New York City, but raised on Long Island. My parents moved to Huntington when I was very young. By age 7, I was playing football, basketball, baseball, and soccer year round. I often dreamed of being a professional football player as a kid. My father was a sports fanatic, and he really pushed me to excel in sports, almost too hard. He was an Army Veteran and a highly decorated New York City firefighter. His personality was ice cold, and I was scared to death of him growing up. Living up to his expectations was something I could never do, even though I got straight A's in school and won numerous awards in sporting events. The pressure would cause me to implode.

On the surface, it seemed like I was a normal, excitable child but nothing could have been further from the truth. There were signs early on that something wasn't right with me. Some people may have even called me deranged. When I was around 10 years old, I bashed my neighbor's head in with a claw hammer and almost killed him. I don't know why I did it, I just wanted to. My personality was extremely shy, anti-social, and almost introverted. At a young age, my dad pushed me very hard to work out with weights and I hated it. But around the age of 16, I started doing it on my own and began building myself

1

up slowly. My teenage years were littered with drug use and acts of juvenile delinquency, a sort of prelude of things to come. I played football up through the 11th grade and was on a Division II championship team at a Catholic high school. The coach of my team would go on to become the Director of Player Personnel for the New York Jets and also a very successful NFL analyst. That would be my final season though. By 12th grade, I had transferred to Walt Whitman High School and completely lost interest in sports. A lot of what ended up changing my mind was that I started smoking pot when I was about 12 years old, and it began changing me. For a long time, I was a jock and lived for sports, but almost overnight I became a burn out who became more interested in getting high and skipping school. I am sure my parents had much bigger aspirations for me than to become a dangerous drug-dealing gangster or hood, but that is exactly what I would grow up to be. The term hood is kind of an old-fashioned way to describe a criminal. Things were about to get very interesting.

For some unexplainable reason, I started to become more and more rebellious the older I got. By age 18, I had two years of karate training under my belt, which would come in handy with the crowd I was starting to hang around with. In the summer of 1984, I started experimenting with anabolic steroids. Between my temper, my rebellious attitude, and the 'roid rage brought on by the steroids, something bad was going to happen. It was all a recipe for disaster.

I'll never forget the night I took my first steroid injection. Standing with me on the side of my house was this drug-dealing thug named Ira "Finster Baby" Kilstein, his nickname coming from the Bugs Bunny cartoon character who was always playing with the dirty money. Kilstein was an obnoxious bastard who rubbed everyone the wrong way. The only thing more offensive than Kilstein's attitude was the foul odor that emanated from his mouth. He had the breath of a tyrant. He also had a reputation as a big bully and was a heavy steroid user. I can't believe I let him talk me into taking steroids. That night the full moon bathed the concrete on the side of my house with a warm glow, and gave my neighbors next door a great view of me pulling down my pants. It was around 9 P.M. Kilstein looked at me with this evil grin on his face and said, "Drop 'em." I did just that, and he pulled out two syringes that looked more like harpoons. He gave me a shot of testosterone and a shot of Winstrol. And boy did that shit work fast. Within weeks I was noticeably bigger and much stronger.

I was working out with my friend's brother, Jake Armstrong, with the weights and karate and had been for some time. Jake Armstrong was a maniacal, tightly wound Irishman with a propensity for violence. Without much of an education, he was drawn to a life of crime like a moth to a flame. Jake and I, along with our other pals, were beginning to fight a lot and started to develop quite a reputation. We had wrecked a bunch of bars in town and were becoming a real thorn in almost everyone's side. We were quite the restless and angry horde. The Huntington Village was the scene of some of our best bar brawls.

I can distinctly remember one Friday night that summer that I was home watching TV when I received a call from Jake. He was at a party in Northport with two girls when a bunch of punks started hassling him. When he left the party, he dropped the girls off and shot over to my house. The both of us were spoiling for a fight. After getting me, we picked up three more guys who would turn out to be useless when the shit hit the fan. The five of us drove back to the party and went looking for them. When we arrived at the house, we parked down the street.

We hadn't even made it up the driveway when one of those punks came out of the house with his hands up challenging us. Without hesitating, I stepped forward and launched a perfect front kick, nailing him square in the balls. The man was lifted five feet in the air. When he crashed to the pavement, everyone started kicking him repeatedly like a bunch of wolves on a fresh kill. He managed to squirm away with ruptured testicles and ran back inside the house. That's when the real shit went down.

Wham! The front door to the house was flung open and a dozen guys with bats and assorted weapons charged down the driveway at us. Two of the chickens I was with immediately turned tail and ran away up the block for the car leaving Jake, Bobby, and me to try to fend off twelve attackers with weapons. The house was in this heavily wooded area where there were no streetlights at all. It was almost pitch black. Jake and I backed up carefully into the street as the twelve guys surrounded us.

With only scant beams of moonlight sneaking in through the treetop canopy, I could barely make out the dark figures circling us. Neither group of men made the first move until I heard Jake scream out "Pat, look out!" I leaned forward and some guy behind me took a swing at my head with an aluminum baseball bat. Just as he swung and missed, Jake nailed the guy with a metal lawn chair, hitting him over the head and knocking him unconscious. I grabbed the guys' bat, and Jake and I went on a fucking rampage in the darkness dropping bodies. You could hear the ding of the aluminum bat each time I connected with either bone or flesh. We dropped eight of the twelve guys who attacked us. The rest of their crew cut their losses and ran like a bunch of scared rabbits. After mauling the shit out of them, we hopped back into Jake's car and split. When we were pulling away from the scene, we could see all those guys laid out in the street barely moving. It was quite invigorating. Jake and I really ripped the other guys who were with us for running away. Hey, the way we looked at things was that you stick together, no matter the odds. If we take a beating, we do it together. Word of the chaotic fight spread like a forest fire all through Huntington, and by now everyone began taking notice. We had become extremely dangerous. It was now 1985, and Jake and I had begun working out five days a week with Master Richie Barathy of American Combat Karate. When the year started, we were all working menial labor jobs, but that wouldn't be for long. One thing would end up changing everything…Cocaine. In no time, my friends and I would hang ten and ride the tidal wave of cocaine importation as it splashed ashore and became the faces of the modern day gangsters in America.

It was during this time while working for a landscaper named J.P. that I came up with an idea. My friends and I were busting our asses living paycheck to paycheck. So me being an ambitious guy decided to find a way to boost our earnings. J.P. was a business owner but was also a cocaine dealer. I went to him and explained my idea to start selling coke and asked if he could front me an eight ball to get started. J.P. liked my idea and agreed to do so.

Cocaine was everywhere by 1985. At first I knew very little about it except what using it felt like. But I would be a quick study. Starting off, I partnered up with some guy named Kip "Scar" Santiago who was going to help me move the stuff. We called Kip "Scar" because there was a long five-inch scar above his left eyebrow that he got in some fight where he got hit with a tire iron. Measuring in at barely 5'7, he was your quintessential punk. He had a real loud mouth but was all bark and no bite, like a human Chihuahua. So that weekend Kip and I threw a little get together at his father's house to get the ball rolling. We split the eight ball, which was 3.5 grams, into half-gram packages. Once all the guests arrived, we told everyone that we were now in business. Soon after the first lines were laid down on the table, our supply was bought up within the hour. Shit, it was the easiest money I ever made in my entire life. When the last package was sold, Kip and I called J.P. and bought two more eight balls. They were sold over the next few hours. We were in disbelief in how quickly the money turned over. I had no clue that we had just opened Pandora's box.

From that point on, things started cooking. My training partner Jake wanted in on this hustle and within weeks would replace Kip as my dealing partner. Cocaine and crack cocaine had been around for a while now and were surging through the New York area. Almost everyone I knew was using cocaine or crack cocaine. What was scary was that jocks and preppies that swore off drugs were becoming involved in the use of cocaine.

With business booming, Jake and I needed a bigger supplier for the amounts we were going through. Our business literally exploded overnight so we now needed a connection for kilos of cocaine. Someone at the gym and karate school we were working out at ended up introducing us to a guy named Todd O'Connor, who was from Bellmore, New York, on the South Shore of Long Island. Todd had a hookup in Jackson Heights, Queens, with some Colombians who were part of some major cartel. This was perfect for us.

Following the introduction to Todd, we all hit it off right away. He was definitely our kind of people, which was nuts. Todd only sold cocaine on the side. His real job was being a member of a robbery crew called "The Crash and Carry Gang" better known to the FBI as The Francois Organization. A maniac named Robyn Francois led the Gang. They would rob stores by ramming a truck through a storefront window and loot as much merchandise as they could before taking off. They were not subtle in their methods. Using police scanners and lookouts was part of the way they operated.

Geraldo Rivera did a TV special in 1991 that told of the insane heists they pulled off. There were interviews on the TV show with some of the FBI agents who had been trying to build a case against the organization. Geraldo showed captured video footage from a home movie Francois made, where he is standing in a room full of stolen TVs and stereos with Todd O'Connor. In it, both of them were wearing New York City police uniforms and were bragging that it took them six hours to sledgehammer through a wall at Crazy Eddies. Francois and O'Connor were laughing in the video, mocking the police. The gang led authorities on some dangerous high-speed car chases reminiscent of the one in the movie The French Connection. These men knew no fear whatsoever. Eventually our coke business and theirs would overlap.

Within weeks, we met another member of the gang who was a lot younger than the others. He went by the name of Chris Campanella. Standing at 5 foot 11 inches, 180 pounds, Chris was another lunatic from Bellmore, who was the youngest member of the gang. Robyn Francois and Todd O'Connor would groom Chris in their smash and grab schemes. Chris was a collegiate wrestler who had the heart of a lion, and he loved mixing it up as far as fighting went. They proved to be worthy allies. Jake and I ended up hanging out with them after we did our coke deals with Todd. For a while, it was kind of fun.

Back in Huntington, things were getting intense. So many people were now being affected by the cocaine and crack epidemic that it was scary. And it wasn't just here in New York. Cocaine and crack were taking their tolls on families all over this country. Jackson Heights, Queens, was now the cocaine capital of the country. It wasn't unusual to turn on the nightly news and see busts as large as 500 or 1,000 kilos in the New York area regularly.

Friends of mine started dropping like flies, having had their lives destroyed by using cocaine. Stories began to emerge of people doing unbelievable things to get the stuff. A buddy of mine, who shall be nameless, started smoking the rock, which is slang for crack, gave another man a blow job in the Fulton Street parking lot for a lousy $20 piece. Man, that's hitting rock bottom. I was at a party one night and watched some girl, who for a half gram of coke let this guy take all kinds of liquor bottles and ram them up her ass. Another girl let a dozen guys pull a train on her right on the front lawn of the party in front of everyone. She got an eight ball for her performance. It was horrible seeing what this white powder was making people do. The more time passed, the worse the stories got.

There was nothing like cracking open that first kilo of cocaine. Jake had gone into Jackson Heights and picked up two kilos, one for each of us. His nerves were shot after driving home looking over his shoulder the entire 30-minute trip. The kilos were in the shape of almost a good size book. Its first outer layer was like a wax paper with the cartel stamp on it. The stamps were black scorpions. After ripping that off, there were super thick layers of saran wrap. There was grease in between some of the layers. Finally, there was a piece of inner tube from a tire snuggly wrapped around the coke. What was left was a glistening 2.2-pound brick of the cartel's finest that reeked of kerosene. It was the purest stuff you could get, and it was right off the boat from Colombia. Our customers went crazy over the shit. It was great for sniffers, but also came back 100 percent rock when you cooked it for smoking. We now had the best cocaine in town. In fact, it was so good we called it truth serum.

On a typical night, I would sit at my kitchen counter top with my triple beam scale and the cocaine in the fridge. There were no cell phones yet, so I would wait for my beeper to go off, then call the person back from my rotary dial phone, and have them stop by my house. The house was like a McDonald's drive through starting around 5 P.M. and would remain open sometimes as late as 6 A.M.. The money was pouring in by now, and my bank account was growing. Almost every night there were cars lined up from my house stretching to the end of my block. It was amazing. Hey, those customers wanted the best, and I had the best.

The neighbors took a while to catch on to what was happening. When they finally figured it out, they didn't like it one bit. After two or three months, my neighbors had seen enough. A lot of them started calling the police almost daily, desperately trying to put a stop to the insanity that was taking place on Horton Drive. Some called due to jealousy because they had to go to work every day and were barely getting by, while I was this 19-year old kid sitting home and raking in obscene amounts of money without working at all. Jake and I were each making between $5,000 and $10,000 a week tax-free. For being average kids from the suburbs, that was serious dough. And we were just starting to scratch the surface of this modern-day gold rush.

Sometimes in life the direction you choose could come down to making a choice that at the time didn't seem like a big deal, only looking back you knew it wasn't smart. Had my conversation gone differently with my father in the spring of 1985, I may never had become a criminal. While shooting hoops with my old man that breezy afternoon in April, we struck up a conversation. I had been kicked out of Walt Whitman High School a few months earlier but had been working full-time ever since. He was kicking my ass in the game of Horse when I asked if he would co-sign a loan for me so I could get a new Mustang GT. Scowling, he told me in his usual nasty tone, to take that idea and stick it. Feeling dismissed, I looked him right in the eye and said, "Oh yeah, watch me get it anyway." I was working hard at the time and would have kept at it, but his rejection and the way he did it burned me badly. I don't blame him for me becoming a criminal, but that was the final straw. Somehow, I was determined to find a way to get it. Selling cocaine would help me achieve that. That's when I began hustling. Not even two months later, I rolled into my driveway in a brand new, sleek, black and grey Mustang GT with centerline rims. My father was so stunned his jaw hit the floor. He just stood there shaking his head in utter amazement. He was clueless as to how I pulled it off, but soon enough he would begin to see the light.

Cocaine was the big thing in the disco scene in the 1970s, but that was nothing compared to what was happening in the 1980s. Cocaine and now crack cocaine were hitting every avenue of American life. Its use was spreading like a virus that was now totally out of control, and the casualties were starting to mount up. It seemed like everyone knew someone who had died or was in rehab due to these drugs. Even the smallest towns in America were dealing with their own horrors from this drug epidemic. Here in New York, it was moving at an unrelenting pace. Kids as young as ten to twelve years old were doing this shit. Teachers, lawyers, firemen, and even cops were getting high on cocaine. You want to know what the hottest selling commodity on Wall Street was, Colombia's finest, and I am not talking about the coffee. For the next year, the good times would roll as far as business went, but Jake and I did a lot more than sell drugs, we trained like animals.

Having an opportunity to train with Master Richie Barathy in American Combat Karate was without a doubt one of the greatest things in life I have ever done. To say he was incredible would be an understatement. He had black belts in seven different styles and was known all over the world for his unique abilities. Master Barathy in the mid-1960s started his martial arts career in a hard-core system called Nisei Goju in Manhattan's Alphabet City. Following his time there, he began training in at least six other styles in the arts. In the early 1970s, he put them all together and formed his own style that was called American Combat Karate. Barathy became a household name in karate by the mid-1970s, and was making regular appearances on all the latest TV shows at that time doing demonstrations and displaying his awesome power when breaking granite. On the Johnny Carson show, his arm caught fire while attempting to smash a dozen flaming granite slabs. All the exposure enabled him to open the first of two popular gyms and karate schools on Long Island. The gym was called RABs Health Club with the other half being called American Combat Karate. Some of the biggest names in bodybuilding and power lifting trained there, guys like Jimmy Quinn and Jimmy Pellechia. The gym was a weight lifter's dream, and people trained like animals there. Master Barathy also trained professional athletes.

Both Jake and I had about two years' experience in the arts before we trained with Master Barathy. But those schools were a joke compared to what we were now doing with him. American Combat Karate was a school of hard knocks, and to learn you were going to take a lot of punishment. It was bare feet and bare knuckle all the way. My first lesson with him was rough. I ended up burning all the skin off the bottom of my feet from the wood floor. But I was back in the saddle the next week with fresh calluses on my feet and was good to go.

One of our first sparring sessions with him, he beat the crap out of Jake and me pretty good. Jake had a bruise on his chest in the shape of a perfect footprint. Master Barathy wanted to see if we had any heart, and he got his answer the following day when we came back for more. This began a long-time friendship between us, and we began a routine that had us training together three hours a day, five days a week. Over the next few years, our abilities as far as fighting went gigantic leaps forward. As green belts, we were beating the shit out of black belts from other schools. Barathy was one of the top Martial Artists in the world, and his ability as an instructor was legendary. All you had to do was watch one of his classes with his students, and you would be able to draw the conclusion that this guy just did things at a different level. Once Jake and I were done training with him each day, we concentrated on business. Sometimes at night we would go out to bars to pick up women or just blow off steam. This is where most of our troubles happened.

On a chilly Thursday evening in mid-October 1986, a bunch of our buddies had gone down to the Huntington Village to a club called Heartbounds. It was a place where they allowed all kinds of people who were underage to come in to drink. The music was loud, the women were hot, and the young men roamed in packs trying to get lucky or start a fight. Most of the bars in the Huntington Village were like that, but this one was especially rowdy. Two of our friends, who were also business associates, ended up getting jumped and beat up by a group of about twenty guys when they left the club that night. Word got back to Jake and me later that night, but it was too late. By the time we went back there, everyone was gone. The next day, we got word of who some of the guys were who did a number on our pals. A little payback was in order.

That Saturday night around 8 P.M., about thirty of our friends congregated at Jakes' parents' house. Most of the guys in our crew were sizeable and were heavy weight lifters. This was going to get ugly for somebody. Everyone was angry, and people were pacing back and forth anxiously. After getting the address of a couple of brothers who beat our friends down, we devised a plan. A good portion of our crowd had weapons. Jake and I both grabbed 12 gauge shotguns and briefed the group on our plan to assault the brothers at their own house. We would deal with the others later on. Before leaving, Jake and I put on our raiding gear. Now clad in black hooded sweatshirts and dark sunglasses, Jake and I motioned for all to follow us, and we jumped into about ten cars and left. This looked like a scene right out of the movie, "The Warriors."

The brothers' house was on a small street off New York Avenue by St. Hugh's Church. I am sure the last thing on their minds was running into us on their own doorstep. Very quietly, all ten cars rolled up in front of the house, and we all hopped out. Someone began pounding on the door, but no one answered. I said, "Fuck it. Let's wreck the place." On cue, the ghouls I was with began throwing boulders through the windows of the house. They broke every one of them. Jake and I grabbed our shotguns and began pumping buck shot rounds and slugs through the two cars in the driveway. We then turned around and put another ten rounds in the house. After that, we flipped the cars onto their roofs. Everyone was going fucking berserk. What we didn't know was that the two brothers were home, cowering under a table. They would have been killed had they answered the door. The wilding lasted a good ten minutes. With no one to hurt, we began losing interest and decided to leave. Police arrived on the scene about five minutes after we left. After that night, no one would ever think of fucking with any of us again. We had become full-fledged gangsters in a very short period of time. But the police would finally learn our names, and that wasn't a good thing. There is nothing a cop hates more than a violent drug dealer. In hindsight, it was pretty stupid getting involved in trivial things like that because we should have been avoiding the spotlight altogether while dealing drugs. But we were young, brash, fearless, and couldn't give a flying fuck.

While our crew was busy tearing up this section of Long Island, New York City was literally burning to the ground. Drugs and violence fueled it all. The city was a giant mass of urban decay, and certain areas of New York City looked worse than Germany after it was bombed out during World War II. It was a war zone, and the streets ran red with blood. People were killing each other at an alarming rate. Two incidents I recall would really signify the time that was New York City in the 1980s. One was a mass murder that became known as the Palm Sunday Massacre.

On April 15, 1984, a crack addict who went by the name of Christopher Thomas would break into an apartment at 1080 Liberty Avenue in the East New York section of Brooklyn. He thought that some cocaine dealer who was living there was banging his woman. Thomas decided to dish out his own twisted version of justice. As it turns out, the dealer wasn't home that fateful day Christopher Thomas decided to drop by. However, eleven innocent women and children were. There were two female adults and nine children all sitting around watching TV. Thomas, now cracked out of his mind, burst into the apartment and in heinous fashion began shooting everyone inside. He didn't stop until ten bodies were scattered throughout. In all, there were two women and eight children murdered with cruel disregard for human life. Miraculously, one of the babies who was shot survived the ordeal. When police arrived at the scene, they were shocked at the brutality. Thomas was arrested soon after and was eventually convicted. It was the largest mass murder at the time in the tri-state area. And yes, drugs were a driving force in this pure act of evil.

Before going into the second incident, let me set the stage as to what the city was like. Cocaine, crack, and heroin had completely taken over most of the inner-city neighborhoods. By 1985, neighborhoods such as the South Bronx, Harlem, Jamaica, and North Brooklyn had become overwhelmed with drugs. Most of these areas had become open-air drug markets with dealers lining up on almost every single street competing in this highly profitable hustle. Abandoned buildings would have lines of people by the hundreds, stretching for blocks like it was the opening of some blockbuster movie, all waiting to cop drugs in the open. People flocked from all over the tri-state area into the hood, so they could get the best product for the cheapest price. The turnover rate was monumental and with all of this wheeling and dealing going on, it was destined to bring in another bad element. There were certain criminals who started seeing an opportunity to cash in on this. Dealers began getting robbed all the time by stick-up men. This caused a huge spike in the homicide rate and violence overall. This was a real cutthroat business where only the strong survived. You had to be ruthless as a dealer if you wanted to stay in business. In 1984, the NYPD launched operation "Pressure Point" to try to combat these dope spots.

Now the next incident I was referring to was an unbelievable story that went down in the South Bronx. As I mentioned before, the amount of drug-related killings was staggering. In a few such cases that took place in the South Bronx and Manhattan, a homicide unit wanted to question a man who they believed was involved in as many as seven execution-style murders of known drug dealers. The suspect was a 20-year-old male named Larry Davis. Davis was a career criminal with a long rap sheet. This is where the epic showdown begins.

On the night of November 19, 1986, a group of thirty officers from the Elite Emergency Services Unit stormed the housing project where Larry Davis' sister lived. Davis had been lying low there. The cops proceeded to boot the apartment door in, unaware as to what awaited them. Not knowing there were children inside, the police rushed in with assault rifles and shotguns ready to fire. Larry Davis was in the back bedroom when he heard them come in. As soon as they saw Davis, the cops started firing at him. Davis pulled back and began to wildly return fire with a shotgun and a few pistols. He was armed with a sawed off 16-gauge shotgun, a .45 caliber pistol, a .32 caliber pistol, and a 357 magnum. As Larry Davis blazed away in his best gangster style, an incredible and lengthy gun battle ensued that would completely destroy the apartment. All in all, six police officers were shot, and three of them had half of their faces blown off. What happened next was just ridiculous. Somehow, Davis managed to dive out the bedroom window while there were now hundreds of cops roaming the perimeter. Larry took a running start and jumped a fence with some very dangerous pit bulls inside the fence. Davis disappeared into the night, and one of the greatest manhunts in the State of New York began.

With almost every law enforcement officer looking for Davis this side of the Mississippi, calls began flooding in on his whereabouts. There were reports within days that Larry Davis was now dressed up as a woman. Huntington, where I lived, was one of the places he was supposedly hiding. In all, Davis would be on the run for seventeen days until he was finally tracked down to a Bronx apartment building. On the 14th floor, Davis was holed up in someone's apartment, trying to secure a safe surrender to the FBI. Larry was afraid the NYPD would shoot him onsite for what he had done weeks earlier, shooting those other cops. After his arrest, Davis claimed that he was dealing drugs for a bunch of dirty cops where he lived in the Bronx, and he believed they were coming to execute him on the night of the 19th. This could have been true because the New York City Police Department was rife with corruption on almost every level back then. And the police were the ones who opened fire first when they entered the apartment. Davis was charged with six counts of attempted murder for shooting the cops and would also face weapon charges and charges of murder of the few drug dealers.

Due to the high profile status of the case, the super famous civil rights attorney William Kunstler decided to defend Davis. It would become one of the biggest and most important cases of the late 20th century. There were a few reasons for this. First, it would shine a spotlight on the way police operated in minority areas and their mistreatment of minorities in the ghetto. It would also open a lot of eyes as to police corruption, which was becoming totally out of control due to the large amounts of money circulating from the drug trade.

Now the cases wouldn't go to trial for some time. While Davis was being held on the infamous Riker's Island jail, the guards were brutalizing him. There were attempts on his life, and there was a strong reason to believe the police were behind it all. Almost every time Davis was brought into court, one of his arms was broken. These incidents seemed to make Davis' earlier claims seem that much more valid. There was no doubt the cops were out to get him. This only helped fuel Kunstler's defense that something serious was being covered up. And when the trial started, Kunstler leaned heavily on this theory to make his case.

After a long trial, where the District Attorney paraded all the police officers that were shot as witnesses for the prosecution, the case was finally in the hands of the jury. The waiting for the jury to deliberate was agonizing for the city. On one side, you had the cops and pro police supporters who wanted to have Davis' head on a stake, and on the other side was the anti-establishment and people in the hood who wanted Davis to beat what was considered a corrupt system. The verdict was "Not Guilty" on all attempted murder charges of the cops who were shot. The boys in blue were flat out stunned. It wasn't over, though. Davis was eventually convicted on weapons charges and received a five to fifteen year sentence. Larry Davis became a symbol of someone who stood up to the system. He was later killed in prison, and to this day is looked at as some kind of folk hero to the people in the hood.

Now back to my story on Long Island. After we destroyed that house and shot it up, the police took us very seriously. They didn't know how to handle the type of situation they saw evolving. There wasn't a lot of experience in dealing with gang type crime in the middle-class neighborhoods. We were operating with a swagger that no one in these parts had ever seen. The Suffolk

County Police actually enlisted the aid of some officers from New York City's gang unit to help with the problem.

The week after we trashed that house, a close friend of mine named Ted was eating lunch in his kitchen when he heard the doorbell ring. Ted was also a dealer. To his surprise, he opened the door and saw three detectives standing there. They began questioning him about the night we all wrecked that house. Now Ted was smart and one of my closest friends, so he wasn't going to give them anything they could use. The cops tried threatening him, saying they had a witness who put him at the scene and got his license plate. Ted never took the bait. He was studying to become a lawyer, so they would have to do a better job if they wanted to trip him up. When they started asking who was selling drugs, Ted started laughing at them. He bid them farewell and slammed the door in their faces. The police left extremely angry. What we didn't know at the time is that they went right back to the precinct and started their first investigation into us.

As 1986 turned into 1987, the President's first lady Nancy Reagan's "Just Say No" campaign was in full swing. Just Say No was a nationwide program aimed at brainwashing kids, starting at the elementary school level to abstain from using drugs. So as her program was starting to take effect on the youngsters, our Just Say Yes mission was hitting on all cylinders with the older crowd. It's hard to believe just how many people were getting high on everything from marijuana to cocaine to heroin. And my boys and I were reaping the rewards.

Our organization, or hierarchy, broke down to something like this. There were around twenty to thirty of us who hung around together, and almost all of us dealt drugs or were involved in some type of criminal activity. Jake and I were absolutely in charge. We supplied everybody with everything. All of our subordinates feared us to death because Jake and I were by far the most violent of the crew. Jake stood 6 feet tall and weighed about 200 pounds. He was shredded with an incredible muscular physique. Jake had almost male model looks, with long flowing blonde hair, and piercing blue eyes. But don't let that fool you because he was one mean hombre. I, on the other hand, was 5 foot 11 and 225 pounds of bulky muscle. My hair was long and brown, and I sported a thick mustache. What was unique was that my eyes were grey. Jake and I were an extremely frightening tandem to be around, and we were known for our insane tempers. There were more than a few examples of what happened when either one of us blew a gasket.

We were both hanging out one night at a local bar on Route 110 in Huntington called the London Pub. We were minding our own business, when some good looking flirty woman started hanging around us looking for attention. Deciding to have a little fun, we began joking around with her. There was this guy who had been trying to pick her up that we did not notice at first. He became jealous when her attention shifted to us. This would create a problem.

Feeling uncomfortable from all the smoke in the bar, I asked Jake if he wanted to bounce. He said yes, and we walked outside to the parking lot. Surprisingly, we ran into three guys who we went to school with. As the five of us were catching up, that woman from the bar came up to us and again began flirting. The conversation went back and forth, and I said something joking around to her. Right then I heard a voice behind me yell, "You owe her an apology." When I turned around, it was the same jealous guy from inside the bar. He stood 6 foot 4 and weighed about 250 pounds. I got right in his face and said, "Fuck you." He flinched, and I drilled him in the stomach with a front kick and sent him tumbling backwards into a car bumper. Thinking he would be smart enough to walk away, I turned my back on him. That was stupid. It could have cost me my life. Suddenly, there was a click and someone yelled, "He's got a knife." As I spun around, this motherfucker lunges at me with this big ass blade. Before I had a chance to move, Jake roundhouse kicked the knife from the guy's hand. Jake then hit him in his left eye with a right hook, and the guy's eyelid tore open. Raging mad, I grabbed the guy and threw him up against the brick wall by the entrance to the bar. After knocking him down, I began hitting him in the face with front kicks repeatedly. Every time my foot connected, his head hit the wall. I must have kicked him a dozen times. His forehead split wide open, and blood was pouring out all over the concrete. He toppled over unconscious and wasn't moving. The guys in the parking lot were in shock at how savagely we beat him. Holy shit, the guy looked like he had just come through an interrogation at the Hanoi Hilton.

Minutes later, patrons from the bar came out to see what all the commotion was about. I grabbed the knife to keep as evidence in case I got into trouble if the guy died. Jake and I left in his car, and the three other guys we knew split in a hurry. We stopped by my father's house to give him the knife to hold onto just in case. My poor father was woken up in the middle of the night only to hear of our close call. At this point, nothing surprised my Dad.

Jake and I drove back by the pub and saw a parking lot with at least five cop cars, two detective cars, and an ambulance. From a distance, we tried to figure out what was going on. Taking a deep breath, I said, "Shit, this can't be good." Having all those cops there was not a good sign. Word spread quickly that someone was killed in a bar fight. The reason people thought this was because the paramedics could not revive him at the scene. But they did so on the way to the hospital. The guy who tried to stab me ended up living but had some brain damage. Me, I couldn't care less. That piece of shit got what he had coming. Either way, we were making too much money to be getting involved in these situations. The bars were loaded with drunken assholes and idiots all wired up on cocaine so it would serve us best to avoid them. Our sins were mounting by the day, and we were flirting with a 20-year jail sentence on a regular basis. Six months later, Jake and a few of the boys wrecked that same bar in an old fashioned western saloon style bar brawl.

Back in 1985, I had a customer who owed me $700. Steroided out at the time, my temper was down right nasty. One afternoon while I was in a bad mood, this guy came by on the wrong day wising off to me. And he didn't have my cash. He shot off his mouth like a tough guy so I grabbed him by his hair. I jammed my thumb into his left eye and crushed it. As it penetrated, it felt like I was pressing through a hard boiled egg with loose yolk behind it. Fluid from his eye ran down my forearm. It was gruesome. Long story short, he got a glass eye, and I got my money. Drug dealing and the violence that went along with it were paramount.

Settling into a nice routine, we began expanding the scope of our business. In addition to selling cocaine, we were now selling steroids, pain pills, other pharmaceuticals, and even small amounts of marijuana. And we also began some small loan sharking. Nothing really on a mob type level, but we were drawing a profit from it. Things were now moving fairly smoothly most of the time. By now, both Jake and I collected a lot of booty along the way. No, I don't mean ass, I mean another type of booty. I'm talking about things people would come to barter with to either clear up a debt or trade outright. And we were stockpiling the stuff. Sometimes we would hold things for collateral, but we usually ended up keeping it. We all had multiple luxury cars, motorcycles, dirt bikes, and many other expensive worldly possessions. Most of the time I never cared about taking things from people, but one guy came along and changed the way I looked at things.

I met this Italian guy named Chuck through a mutual friend named Scotty, who was a bass player who I jammed with from time to time. Chuck was a few years older than me and was a real stud with the ladies. He dated some of the hottest girls imaginable. Most of us were jealous of his conquests. He started buying half ounces of coke from me, which went on for quite a while. A year later, he came over to my house with a tanning bed, looking for credit. It was worth about a grand. I liked Chuck so I said, "Sure," and gave him an ounce for it. Not long after that, he disappeared for a while. I had not heard from him so I phoned Scotty and asked if he had seen Chuck. Scotty passed along some sad news. Chuck had killed himself. Apparently, he was smoking crack like a fiend and became really depressed. He was found hanging in his closet at home. This was really upsetting because I liked Chuck a lot. This was not the first, and unfortunately, would not be the last person I would know to die from drugs.

My buddies and I were living a super lifestyle. We were eating out three times a day in the best restaurants all over New York City and Long Island. In high-class eateries, such as The Clubhouse in Huntington or Peter Luger's in Great Neck, we had our own tables. Angelo's in Little Italy was my favorite Italian restaurant. Once a week, Jake and I would go there and discuss business. The waiters loved seeing us come in because we tipped well, extremely well. For a $400 to $500 meal, we would leave a $400 to $500 tip. We had it going on like that. Ahh, it was great to be king.

In addition to taking exotic vacations, we also frequented sporting events like New York Knicks games or boxing matches. Most of us were sports fanatics, so whenever we went to the games, we always got courtside tickets. It was expensive, but worth every penny. I must have seen Michael Air Jordan play a good ten times. My closet was filled with every pair of Air Jordan sneakers ever made along with the finest clothes money could buy. Football was my sport. Most of my buddies liked the New York Jets or the New York Giants. Not me, I was a die-hard Kansas City Chiefs fan. Down the road I would eventually get to meet the entire Chiefs team. I'll get to that later.

Of all the perks that came along with being in the position we were now in, that of being major drug dealers, the women were the things I enjoyed most. Actually, most of my pals did too. For some reason women couldn't control themselves when it came to cocaine. They would do the wildest things to get it. So being a major coke dealer, I often found smoking hot babes throwing themselves at me in order to get it. My friends used this to cash in and sleep with as many women as they could. It was fun for a while, but eventually it got stale for me. I yearned for something more. So as fate would have it, someone would end up dropping right into my lap.

In March of 1987, while I was home dealing one night, I got a phone call from one of my customers. It was a girl named Vanessa who wanted to come by for an eight ball of blow. She was drop dead gorgeous. Vanessa was half Mexican and half Italian and had the looks and features of a super model. As I opened the door, she came into my house with this big smile on her face that lit up the room. I smiled back, and we began some small talk. After about five minutes of chit chat, she looked at me and said, "I don't just come here for this. I also come here to see you." I was stunned. The wind was almost knocked out of me, and I got weak in the knees. Looking nervous, I was at a complete loss for words. Luckily for me, she did all the talking and asked me out. I could barely get the word "yes" out of my mouth. We had our first date the next weekend, and before I knew it, I was in my first major relationship.

It took off like a rocket ship. I found myself in unchartered waters and definitely wasn't used to having a significant other. Early on, we couldn't get enough of each other and were together 24/7. It was a nice change from my usual isolation. We had sex anywhere and everywhere. Planes, trains, movie theaters, and even restaurant bathrooms were the places we chose to fornicate spontaneously. She was so beautiful, and I was proud to be seen with her. I felt like a king, and every good king needs a queen, and now I had mine.

Now Vanessa was only 18 years old then, but appeared and carried herself much older. She became a gangster's woman and really enjoyed the spot she found herself in. I bought her all the nicest jewelry and the most expensive clothing her heart desired. This was a lifestyle she could only have dreamt of before she met me. We enjoyed each other's company, and would often take long drives upstate or down to the beach. Vanessa would sing along as we blasted the radio. It was 1987, and the music scene was getting big. Whitney Houston, Madonna, and Michael Jackson were dominating the pop charts. I liked all music, but rock and roll was my favorite. The group Van Halen was the ultimate band. Being a guitar player, I idolized Eddie Van Halen. He was like a god to me. Van Halen had been on top of the rock world since 1978.

As big as all this was, it would be a new style of music that would change the music industry forever. It was called Rap, or Hip-Hop, and it would become the soundtrack of what became known as the cocaine wars during the

1980s and 90s. A group called Run DMC was the first one that made it mainstream. Their style was fresh, and the music was cutting edge and captured the pulse of an energetic city. Run DMC paved the way for other up and coming artists such as LL Cool J, Ice T and eventually, the king of them all Jay-Z. These rappers often rhymed about what was going on in the hood and through their lyrics you could often hear strong political statements being made about the current situations. I loved it and became a Hip-Hop fanatic. All over New York City and Long Island, you could hear this music being cranked from boom boxes, which were big, portable box-like stereos. This music went hand in hand with the events going on in the country.

Music was a big part of Vanessa's and my relationship. Even though she was young, she loved the club scene. Clubs were big in the 1980s. Lots of dance music, lots of alcohol, and all the drugs your heart desired were available in every one of them. The 1980's brought new meaning to the expression "powdering your nose." The bathrooms were the most popular places in these clubs because most patrons were in there getting high on cocaine. It was there where Vanessa tried cocaine for the first time. She was hooked immediately. It wasn't long after this that we would eventually meet. Vanessa only lived a few blocks from me, so it was convenient. This is how we eventually met one another. Before we got involved, I didn't have a problem with her doing cocaine, but now that we were a couple and I had strong feelings for her, I started looking at it differently. I was riding a high of spiritual bliss, and realized for the first time in my life I was in love.

This is around the time I started to have a change of heart. To this point, I was a very violent drug dealer and hadn't given much thought to the collateral damage my involvement in the drug trade was causing. Having seen Vanessa wired on coke a few times while we were together, really bothered me. I never thought about the fact that this girl used to be a class president, or cheerleader, but now her life was being deeply affected by drug use. The difference was now I cared. I did my best to get her to stop using once we started seeing each other. I guess it was somewhat hypocritical.

Now this wasn't easy trying to make her stop because she loved the package. Vanessa resorted to sneaking around behind my back to get it. Even though I cut her off, there were plenty of dealers around who she could buy off of. I put the word out that anyone who sells to her, dies. A few days later, she was wired again. With some prodding, I got Vanessa to tell me who sold it to her. It shouldn't have surprised me because this is a cutthroat business, but who sold it to her did. It ended up being my original dealing partner Kip "Scar" Santiago, and he knew better. Backstabbing was commonplace in this kind of work, but he was warned. I left Scar at the starting gate when we started dealing, and he was just a mid-level dealer who I still supplied. Two days later, I caught up to him and gave him and his old man a beating. What he did was an ominous sign of things to come with him. It's this whole fucking lifestyle. People's behavior in the hustle game was shameful, and they were loyal to only one thing, money.

Although I tried to keep somewhat of a low profile, there was just no way to avoid our existence being discovered by the police. The cops, and more importantly, the drug enforcement administration, were on a mission trying to figure out a way to stop the drug crisis gripping our nation. One event ignited the DEA and mobilized them like never before. In 1985 there was a DEA agent named Enrique "Kiki" Camarena, who was working undercover in Mexico trying to take down some high-level figures in a Mexican drug cartel. The cartel found out, and subsequently tortured Kiki for 30 hours before murdering him. This action would prompt a comprehensive investigation that was the largest homicide case in the history of the DEA. They got all the people involved and brought them to justice. This was the thing that seemed to become the driving force to eradicate the drug problem. The DEA usually handled only really large investigations, but due to the damage drugs were causing our country, they would now frequently join forces with local authorities to help combat the problem.

Jake and I had been under surveillance from time to time, and it really didn't bother us. It came with the territory. Spotting a tail, or seeing cops sitting on our houses was relatively easy. To be in this business, you had to constantly be on the lookout if you wanted to remain a free man. The cops looked at our crew as a bunch of young, violent, psychotic, and out of control gangsters with no regard for the law. The police saw us climbing the criminal ladder right in front of their very eyes. They had all kinds of trouble building a case against any of us. I would later find out that the cops actually busted people leaving our houses, but were unsuccessful in obtaining their cooperation. And they tried every trick in the book to get people to roll over on us. The people they caught would just say, "Take me to jail because I'm not answering either to Jake or Patrick."

A good portion of our friends had fairly large gun collections, and everyone knew it. I had a tall gun safe that held an AK-47, an AR-15, a Ruger Mini-14 Ranch Rifle, a .44 caliber and 9MM Uzi, three 12-guage shotguns, and about five pistols. Jake's collection was just as big as mine. This only added to our growing mystique.

Business was great, and it seemed to be getting better. The cocaine side was always steady, and by now all the other stuff we sold was growing. I continued to sell coke, pot, steroids, and pills. The one thing I could have sold but chose not to, was heroin, because I looked at it as taboo. There was always a market for it, only it brought seedier clientele I wasn't willing to gamble on. And the thing I believed most of all is it brought bad karma. Karma is very real, and I would find this out the hard way. I knew people who were doing dope and heard a lot of bad things about it. I was 16 when one of my sister's friends died of a heroin overdose.

Maybe the worst story I ever heard was of another one of my sister's friends named Johnny Butler or Johnny B. Johnny looked like a doper, with sallow skin, sunken in eyes, and weighed about 120 pounds soaking wet. He went into East New York in Brooklyn one day to cop heroin or smack. Somehow he ended up going into a shooting gallery on Euclid Avenue to score. A shooting gallery is usually an abandoned, broken down building where junkies would hole up to get their fix. Johnny bought two bags and went inside, stepping over needles, crack stems, urine, and feces. People were nodding out all over the place. Johnny was only a casual user, so he made a mistake deciding to shoot both bags. The dope was super strong. After injecting the bags, Johnny overdosed and passed out. Now near death, he was a sitting duck. This is where things take a turn for the worse.

There were at least 20 other junkie skells sitting around who took advantage of the situation. First, they robbed him of his wallet with about $300 in it. They also snatched his gold chains and ring. Then came the *coup de gras*. While Johnny was unconscious, four or five of the junkies pulled down his pants and began raping him. To make things worse, they all ejaculated into his rectum. Sometime later, miraculously, Johnny woke up only to find his asshole bleeding, with semen dripping out. He ended up being taken to the hospital and needed surgery. As if things couldn't get worse, he also contracted a few STDs from the assault. These were some of the reasons I avoided Mr. Brownstone.

My marijuana business was now picking up. When I started hustling it, I started only purchasing a pound. I broke it down to quarter pounds and blew it out like that. Fairly quickly, I picked up more and more customers. One pound became two, and then three, and so on. It was easy because nearly everyone I knew smoked pot. Immediately, I saw the potential to make some good cash with this in addition to the cocaine. Needing larger and larger amounts, I needed a serious connection to keep pace with my expansion. Someone at the gym hooked me up with a guy who was known as "Fast" Frankie from Wantagh. Frankie was a short man with blonde hair that looked an awful lot like David Soul from Starsky & Hutch, the TV show. Frankie and I clicked immediately. He was a cool cat.

The first time we did anything, I picked up ten pounds of weed from him. This kept me going for a while. Fast Frankie had been in business for some time. He was either mailing the pot back from Tucson, Arizona, or having runners fly it back on planes after checking their luggage curbside at the airport. His contacts in Arizona were usually Mexican. This was way before 9-11-2001, so it was much easier to smuggle back then. For the amount I was now moving, he was the perfect connect.

Not long after I met Frankie, I met his partner. His name was Charlie Sykes, and people called him Chuck. Chuck was another dwarf, only he had a major attitude problem. Unlike Frankie, who was really cool, Chuck was obnoxious and arrogant, but also well connected. Sykes flaunted his success with a large collection of Porsche automobiles. Although both had differing styles, they both knew how to make money. Sykes was from Roosevelt and spent time between his home here and his pad in Tucson, Arizona. He also owned a few titty bars out there. I would use both guys to get my weed.

As good as things seemed to be going, there would soon be some problems that needed addressing. Business was really rolling, so I should have been cleaning up as far as profits went. I noticed some discrepancies in the books after counting large sums of cash. The money was way short. I am not talking about a few hundred dollars. There were thousands missing. My first thought was that Vanessa might have been stealing from me. I was a trusting person who didn't believe in stealing, so I gave her the benefit of the doubt.

This was my stupidity, though. I kept the cocaine, which was usually a kilo or more in my desk drawer. The reason being if the cops kicked in my door, I had a chance to flush it before they could get to it. I kept money in a safe, but would also leave large amounts of cash in that drawer while doing business. Let's just say I was slightly naïve. Certainly I had seen enough shit already, so I shouldn't have trusted anyone, period. This would be one of those bitter lessons learned.

Early in my dealing career, I hired a friend's sister to come twice a week to clean my house. She did it for a living and loved cocaine so it was a win-win. I should have paid closer attention to what she was cleaning. A hundred dollars cash and an eight ball of coke is what I paid her each week. What I didn't realize is just how bad her cocaine habit was. Two years later, I began to catch on. I should have put it together much sooner. All the evidence was there, I just didn't want to accept that Vanessa might be doing it. However, when it comes to drugs, anything is possible. Sadly, I accused Vanessa and I was wrong.

In August, Vanessa and I were eating dinner late one night at the Clubhouse. After finishing my French silk pie, we paid the bill and left. It was about 11:30 P.M. I don't know what made me think to drive by my house, but I'm glad I did. There, only two houses away, was my house cleaner's car parked in front of my neighbors. Hmmm. Vanessa and I rolled up and parked my Mustang. We quietly crept up to the front door, and I put the key in the lock and unlocked it. I opened the door and screamed, "Who the fuck is there!" Suddenly, I heard footsteps running out the back door. As I entered the house, I heard a crash on the side of the house. Vanessa screamed, "Someone's over here." I ran out to the side and flicked the lights on. There stuck in the sticker bushes and caught on the fence was my housekeeper, dressed in all black like a cat burglar and wearing gloves. I was so angry I could have killed the bitch.

Once I pulled her out of the bushes, I patted her down. On her was a Ziploc bag with a few ounces of cocaine and three grand in cash. The housekeeper was shaking uncontrollably. Even hardened criminals wouldn't have had the balls to try to rob me then. Wow, I did not see this coming. The only question now was what to do with her.

Pissed off, I grabbed the bitch by the hair and dragged her ass inside. I was fuming. She must have gotten me for at least fifty thousand over the last two years. I began contemplating what I should do, so I called Jake. He was in total disbelief. In less than three minutes, he was at my house. Jake cursed the bitch out and recommended we take her to Harlem and sell her to some pimp.

The idea was interesting. In the end, I cut her loose and warned her what would happen if she ever came back. It was the cocaine. It brought out the worst in everyone. Nothing, and I mean nothing, surprised me anymore.

Staying ahead of the police was not all that difficult. Their surveillance techniques and equipment were nowhere near as sophisticated or advanced as they are today. Keeping your own crew in line was a different story though. Most of the people in our circle were a bunch of hoods and hustlers. Independent organizations like ours popped up in every town and every city in this country. All in our circle were criminals to some degree and would all fall for the trappings of easy money. They all lifted weights heavily, and a good portion were into the steroids, or "juice." Competition was fierce amongst the ranks, and there was a constant need for someone to show who the strongest or toughest man was. At 19 years old, I had a 420-pound bench press. Even though they all pumped iron, many had a sweet tooth for drugs. A lot of them would deal to finance their habits and lavish lifestyles. Getting high was a thing that made them vulnerable. You should never break the golden rule, and that is, "Don't get high on your own supply." Too many bad things could happen, and you become extremely sloppy.

At least half of these guys were dealing out of the bars in town. It was a great place to make money but was also very dangerous. When you are drunk, you tend to let your guard down, and in the bars this happens way too much. What the cops would do is send an undercover to hang around the bar to befriend dealers. Next, they would act like they could get you better product for a cheaper price. When not in total control of your faculties, you don't think straight, so before you know it, you are busted on a reverse buy and bust. This happened to a few of the idiots we were dealing with. Unfortunately, this was also a way for the cops to infiltrate the back door of an organization.

Something like this almost happened to Jake one day. While dealing with a 20 year old Asian kid called "Paulie the Gook," Jake made a near-costly mistake. Paulie the Gook was a scatterbrain, who used cocaine intravenously. A black cloud followed him wherever he went. Paulie came to Jake and claimed he knew a guy who had ten pounds of Thai stick marijuana that he wanted to dump for $500 a piece. When something sounds too good to be true, it usually is. When Jake asked me about it, I said, "This sounds fishy to me." I told Jake he would be an idiot to entertain the idea. For Jake, the plum was just too juicy not to take a bite of.

There is no excuse acceptable to warrant Jake doing what he was about to do, except sheer greed. Six hours later, a friend and customer of mine named Brian Bartholameau called me with an interesting story. Brian went on to explain to me that Jake and Paulie the Gook drove to some parking lot in Deer Park to buy the ten pounds of weed. As soon as they pulled in the lot, undercovers swarmed them. It was a total setup. Jake did do one smart thing though, and that was he had someone else in the next parking lot with the money, and they aborted once they saw what went down. The cops blew it as usual and got nothing. Jake was arrested and charged with attempted possession and conspiracy. Nothing ever came of it, and Jake couldn't believe he did something so careless. But a pattern started to develop with Jake taking too many chances. Paulie the Gook was found dead less than a month later in his car with a needle in his arm. He died of a cocaine overdose.

We had a decent run where not too much went wrong, but that would change soon. Both Jake and I continued our heavy-duty training with Master Barathy, and we were becoming very skilled martial artists. Business was good. Both of us were involved in steady relationships with our girlfriends, and that kept us somewhat grounded. There was a wild streak in us though. On occasion, we still liked to go out to the city and do some partying. New York City had always been a dangerous place, and one night I would get a taste of it.

Once a month, some of the boys and I would go out to this club on the Lower East Side of Manhattan. It was called Polyesters, and a buddy of ours named Sean McGuire was a bouncer there. Following a long night of partying there one evening where we all struck out, we left Polyesters and headed to a hooker stroll on Park Avenue to pick up some streetwalkers, or prostitutes. I was ripped. I was drinking tall glasses of Jack Daniels for hours. Pulling up to 23rd and Park Avenue, a few of us got out of the car and began mingling with the ladies of the night. Some guy we called Poncho, and I, each grabbed a girl and split up heading for separate hotels. We were going to meet back at the car when we were done.

My escort took me to some run down fleabag hotel three blocks away. She stood 6 feet 2 and was jacked up. Upon paying the $60 to the creepy clerk behind the desk, he winked at me and smiled. What was that about? The hooker and I walked up the stairs and went in a room. I gave her $200, and we stripped down and started knocking boots. The sex was great, and I nailed her for a good half hour.

Concluding coitus, I grabbed my pants and shirt and got dressed. I checked my pants and noticed that the $1,500 in my pocket was gone. Something made me glance at the garbage pail by the bed. In it was my money. "You fucking bitch," I screamed at the whore. Instead of being afraid I was going to hit her, this crazy ass bitch pulls out a switchblade and swung wildly at me with the knife. Without too much difficulty, I managed to disarm her. She did, however, slash my $300 Italian silk shirt. When I left the room, I headed for the stairs to leave when some 6 foot 3 inch, 300 pound hairy looking biker blocked my exit. He reached behind his back, and I just reacted by hitting him with a sidekick knocking him down the flight of stairs. I bolted from the hotel and went back to the car and headed home. That was one fucked up night.

Jake and I were not the only game in town. We did have a pretty good strangle hold on our area in Western Suffolk County, though. There were two other dealers in town who handled a lot of the run off. One was the bully, Ira Kilstein. The other was a guy named Rich Reikert. Both of them had actually been in business longer than Jake and me. Kilstein was around 6 feet tall and weighted around 275 pounds. He was a big time steroid user and looked like it. Ira was the one who talked me into trying the steroids. Kilstein was also flamboyant and arrogant, two bad qualities for a drug dealer. He flaunted his position and taunted the police.

Boy did Kilstein enjoy starting trouble. He instigated fights among everyone, and I tried to avoid him most of the time. He and I were at opposite ends of the dealing spectrum. I tried to move amongst the shadows, while he practically boasted with a megaphone his business. One afternoon his mouth landed him in some trouble.

He ended up talking some shit about Chris Campanella of the, "Crash and Carry Gang." Jake went back to Chris and told him about it. A few hours later, Campanella met Jake and me at Jake's parents' house and demanded for us to take him over to Kilstein's. The three of us jumped into Jake's pickup truck, and we headed to Ira's. Kilstein came walking outside with his hands up, challenging Chris. He would quickly regret his decision. Chris and Ira began wrestling around, and in about thirty seconds Kilstein was out of gas. He then put his arms around a tree, and while hugging it, screamed for his father to get a bat. Chris teed off and hit him with lefts and rights. After a minute to two, it was over. Kilstein was humiliated. Chris, Jake, and I got in the truck and left. This would cause quite a bit of tension between Jake and Ira for some time.

About a month later, some bad timing would nearly land me in the slammer. Even after the fight, I still tried to remain on good terms with Kilstein. This would come back and bite me. On a beautiful fall afternoon, I decided to drop by Ira's for a workout. I parked my Mustang against the curb in front of his parents' beautiful, L-shaped ranch. I headed into the garage and said, "What up," to Ira. Just as I did my first set on the bench, this guy named Matt Kimblebaum entered the garage. I paid him no mind. He was there to buy cocaine from Ira. Ira then hands him a giant Ziploc bag with nine ounces of coke in it. Kilstein turned his back to count the money while Kimblebaum walked out of the garage and looked toward the street. He held up the bag of blow, as if to show someone. I went over and noticed a Mercedes with a man and woman in it that looked like narcs. I told Ira what just happened and he yelled for Kimblebaum to come back inside. Instead of taking back the product and returning the money, Ira tells him to hide the coke. I said, "Fuck this," and split. His carelessness was something I couldn't comprehend. Kimblebaum left with his counterparts. Nothing happened that day, so Kilstein figured he was in the clear. I knew better. I, on the other hand, was convinced of his fate. Almost a month later, the truth would come out.

While eating out at J&J's Italian restaurant with Vanessa, I got a bad feeling. Five weeks had passed since Kilstein sold to Kimblebaum. I knew not to ignore my gut. We finished eating and got in a rental car I was driving. I sped over to Jake's and skidded on some leaves in front of his house. There was a dark and grey cloudy sky hanging over there that almost warned of the impending doom. I ran up the stairs and into Jake's bedroom. Not two minutes after I had arrived, a guy named Andre B came barreling in, white as a sheep. He was hysterical and rambling so fast we could hardly make out what he was saying. We told him to calm down and take a breath. Finally, he began making sense.

Andre had just come from Kilstein's, and said, "We are all going to jail." He said the DEA had just stormed Ira's house with around twenty agents and that they were still there. Andre was shaken to the core. I warned Jake weeks earlier about what Kilstein did with Kimblebaum. Everyone was unsettled. A few of us then hopped into my rental car and drove by Kilstein's. There were a dozen vehicles in the driveway and street. One was a small, red pickup with two long 8-foot antennas on it. There was also a white van with a spinning antenna on its roof. This was serious shit.

Thinking the worst, we tore ass back to Jake's, and I dropped them all off. As the last person exited the car, we noticed one of the cars that were at Kilsteins was now making repeated passes by Jake's house. We realized how hazardous this situation could potentially become. The previous day, Jake went into Jackson Heights, so we were both sitting on large amounts of cocaine. Jake had three kilos in his house, and I had one and a half. There was also twenty pounds of pot in my friend Randy's garage. Forty-five minutes later I decided to drive by my house to make sure nothing was up. After all, I was at Kilstein's house the day he made the sale to Kimblebaum.

I pulled down the west side of my street in the rental car and was alarmed by what I saw. That red pickup with the antennas, the white van, and two of the other cars that were all at Kilstein's were now parked right in front of my crib. Shit! I didn't even slow down when passing my father's house. This looked bad. Normally nothing fazed me, but this time I was nervous. You couldn't blame me. Under my bed was a kilo and a half of cocaine, and in my closet was a safe loaded with cash and all kinds of illegal goodies. Now, add to that the fact that there were a dozen DEA agents lurking around my property. It was a sphincter-tightening moment. I assumed the Feds were getting ready to boot my old man's door down. This was all because of fucking Kilstein. Why did I have to have the bad luck of stopping by his house when he was making a sale to the Feds that day? Damn, I had to think of something fast.

I drove around the corner to my buddy's Randy's house. Thank God he was home. Randy and I were childhood friends, and I trusted him with my life. I was about to ask him to take another risk for me. Now the DEA must have thought I was home because my Mustang was in my driveway. I told Randy to take my house key, and walk up my street like he was going to stop by to talk to me. Then I asked him to open the front door and run upstairs and flush the coke and split. Randy was not thrilled about my idea. Reluctantly, he agreed to do so. I drove Randy to the end of my block and dropped him off. As he got out of the car, he began sweating bullets.

When Randy was walking down the dark street to my house, his heart began beating faster. His mouth was parched. Seeing the DEA agents' vehicles only raised his anxiety level. He quickly passed the cars and walked up my steps and let himself in. Tiptoeing up the stairs, he noticed my father was in the shower. My poor father had not a clue of the potential legal issues he could possibly be facing had the DEA raided the house. Randy went into my room and grabbed the duffle bag with the cocaine inside. Instead of flushing it, the crazy bastard walked out the back door, hopped the fence, and ran back to his own house. The nerve it took to do that was incredible. I called Randy an hour later, and he told me what he did. I couldn't believe it. Randy claimed he dumped the coke at his house. A month later, he bought a brand new Firebird sports car. I wonder where the money came from?

After settling myself down, I went back to Jake's house and updated him on the situation. He wasn't happy hearing about this. My only worry now was if the Feds were going to hassle my father with this crap. My dad was as straight as they come. He had been a New York City firefighter for the past 27 years, and he hated drugs. I felt terrible about having had put my old man in a potentially compromising situation. In reality, it was all thanks to Kilstein. It's my fault, though. Remember the old saying, "You lay down with dogs, you get fleas." That is exactly what happened here.

Jake and I decided to get hotel rooms out of town for a while until things cooled off a bit. I got a room in Syosset, and Jake grabbed one in Commack. It was time to take a break until the smoke cleared. Me, I had no problem shutting it down, but Jake decided to keep hustling. I recommended he take some time off, but he couldn't stop. He was addicted to making the money. Eventually, there would be consequences for his choice.

Kilstein was indeed arrested by the Feds for a direct sale of a large amount of cocaine. What was puzzling was that he was home the next morning. That was near impossible because processing and arraignment took time. There was only one way he got out that fast, and that meant he rolled over. Rumor quickly spread that he talked so much that the DEA had to slap him to shut him up. Assuming the worst, I avoided him like the plague. Ira didn't appreciate that at all. Kilstein began telling people he was getting off because it was me who made the sale that day to the Feds, not him. He said all four of his family members were witnesses, and they would all testify that I had done it. What a scumbag! That's life in the drug trade. Once the ship starts sinking, it's every man for himself.

This infuriated me when I heard this. I called my lawyer right away and filled him in on everything. He told me to relax. The lawyer came up with a solution. He said I should get Kilstein on tape confessing to the crime. One morning when I was returning home after breakfast, I saw Kilstein on Melville Road on his motorcycle. I pulled him over. In a very sneaky manner, I pulled out a mini recorder, turned it on and started bullshitting with him. I immediately asked him what went down with him. He began lying, so point blank I said, "Why the fuck are you telling people that I was the one who sold the cocaine that day to Kimblebaum?" He replied by saying, "I never said that. I know it wasn't you, I'm the one who did it." Right there I rolled up my window and left. I had my confession.

Not trusting Kilstein, I went back to laying low. Following his release from custody, we started getting followed around all day, every day. It didn't take a genius to realize that Ira Kilstein ratted out everyone in our crew. Still, this didn't bother Jake enough to take a break. He was totally greedy. Hell, we all were, I was just smart enough to know when not to push my luck. The area was flaming hot with law enforcement. The cops would follow us into restaurants, just sit there and stare at us with these really pissed off looks. For now, the only time I would see Jake was in the afternoon at our lessons with Master Barathy. It was there where we would either discuss or do business.

Once Jake noticed the police were staking out his hotel room, he decided to pack up shop and went to Bellmore to stay at Todd O'Connor's house. Our buddy, from the "Crash and Carry Gang," was nice enough to open his home to Jake. So Jake decided to start hustling from there and kept the shop open. By now, Todd had already introduced Jake directly to the Colombians in Jackson Heights. After Todd hooked Jake up, we began seeing less and less of him. That was until now. Todd was a real standup guy, but he was crazy. We always had a lot of fun together whenever we did hang out. Todd was now huge. He had been pumping some serious iron and was also taking steroids. Anyone who has ever taken the "juice," knows it can make you insane. Todd's personality was beginning to change. He became extremely paranoid and restless. Every once in a while, Todd would go on a binge injecting cocaine. Injecting cocaine was by far the most dangerous way to get high if you ask me. Now looking back, it was a terrible idea when Jake ended up going to Todd's to hustle. Jake was at Todd's for about a week.

One snowy night, I slipped my tail and took a cab ride over to Bellmore to Todd's house with Vanessa. The place was a zoo. There were customers of Jake's from Huntington there and a bunch of Todd's buddies from Bellmore and Queens on the premises also. It was extremely loud. This was not what I would call laying low. People were partying with all types of drugs. I said to myself, *This isn't good*. I didn't see Todd, though. Then after about ten minutes, he came out of the bathroom and gave me a big bear hug. Something was off about him. His pupils were dilated, and his eyes were wide as saucers. He was so wired he could barely talk. I looked down and noticed some fresh track marks on his arms. That was disappointing. I've been around people getting high long enough to know when someone starts shooting junk, it becomes a life and death gamble. Todd was a friend, so I voiced my opinion to him. He was babbling and not making sense. I asked Jake to keep an eye on him. Minutes later, I grabbed Vanessa and said, "Let's go." Before we left, I again tried talking Jake into taking a vacation, but it went in one ear and out the other. Vanessa and I called a cab and left.

A half hour later, my girl and I were back at Howard Johnson's hotel and crashed for the night. When we woke up the next morning, I was curious if Jake was going to show up for karate. I called over to Todd's house to talk to Jake, and neither one of them answered. Instead, a low angry voice picked up the phone and said, "Can I help you?" I knew something wasn't right. He asked who I was, so I asked, "Who is this?" To my surprise, he told me it was Detective McCready of the Nassau County Police. Oh no. I asked for Todd, and he replied by saying, "I have some bad news." The Detective told me Todd passed away from what looked like a drug overdose. Hanging up the phone, I was beside myself. Vanessa began crying after I broke the tragic news to her. All of a sudden, I said, "What the hell happened to Jake?" Thoughts of horror began entering my mind. It took a full two days to hear from him. When he finally called, he gave me the 411 on what went on. What a damn shame! Todd was a solid dude, and we would miss him.

Days later, Jake took his girl and left on a two week vacation to Jamaica. I decided to head to California to visit my sister. I hadn't seen my sister since she moved out there two years earlier. We kind of left off on bad terms back in 1985 after I found out she had been robbing me blind of cocaine and selling it to my father's girlfriend. Enough time had passed, so it was water under the bridge. With Vanessa sitting this one out, I headed over to my friend Jobo's house to see if he wanted to take a free vacation. Before I finished asking him, he was standing there with his suitcase ready to go. That night we boarded a United Airways jet bound for San Diego.

When we landed, we had to take a cab ride to my sister's apartment because she was tied up with something. Jobo and I got to her pad thirty minutes later. She lived in Carlsbad. I grabbed the key under the mat and let us in. En-

31

tering the apartment, I noticed a good twenty or thirty shits on the floor that were left by her two small Yorkshire Terriers. Jobo and I then set the kitchen table with plates and silverware. I grabbed a napkin and picked up all the dog shit and split them up evenly and put them on the plates. We then lit a couple of candles and laid down to rest until my sis came home. An hour later my sister and her husband walked in and she said, "Oh Andrew, they cooked us dinner. It looks like sausages." When she got a little closer, she screamed, "Gross!" Jobo and I were dying laughing after my sister realized what it was.

The following morning, we ate breakfast at some fancy place. The weather was magnificent. It was 70 degrees with crystal clear skies. When we were done with our meal, my sister Susan drove us around and showed us some of the local sights. There were palm trees everywhere, and it was so clean, quite a stark contrast to the dreary New York we left the day before. Everything was so different. I fell in love with California as soon as I stepped off the plane. People there took to us right away and were intrigued by our New York accents. Jobo and I found a local gym and started hitting it everyday. Working out was a part of us, and we did it wherever we were. My buddy and I went out drinking at a few clubs the next couple of nights.

Later that week, my sister Susan, her husband Andrew, Jobo, and I drove up to Los Angeles to poke around. It was a shitload of fun. Starting with Beverly Hills, we made our way around to most of the attractions. Over the next three days we took a tour of the movie stars homes, hit Universal Studios, and finally Disneyland. Sometime during that trip, it dawned on me that I wasn't being followed around anymore. I found the stress-free environment quite enjoyable.

While we were there, my sister Susan asked me if I wanted to move out there. I actually gave it some serious thought. But after thinking it over, I realized it would be too difficult at that time. First off, I was deeply in love with Vanessa, and she was too young to be asked to move 3,000 miles away from her parents. Secondly, I had an established business back in New York that was very lucrative. There was no way in hell I was giving that up. Jobo and I stayed in California for a month. When it was up, we were ready to head back east to New York. My sister Susan was sad seeing us leave, but I told her we would be back. And I kept my word. Jobo and I ended up going back two more times to visit.

Jobo and I arrived back at LaGuardia Airport in New York late at night. I grabbed a limousine to take us back to Long Island. The weather was freezing cold and after being in warm, sunny California for a month, we weren't used to these frigid temperatures. On the drive home, I looked out the windows and noticed there were these dark clouds hovering over the area, with bursting flashes of lightning that gave our homecoming quite an eerie feel. Half of me missed California, but the other half was glad to be home. After dropping Jobo off, the limo continued another block and pulled up to my father's house. I tipped the driver well and headed inside. Ah, home sweet home.

Vanessa caught me completely off guard when I opened my bedroom door to find her totally naked in my bed, waiting for me to come home. Looking at each other, our faces lit up simultaneously. We embraced tightly, and neither one of us wanted to let go. I jumped in bed, took off my clothes, and worked her over real well. She could tell by my enthusiasm and appetite that I had missed her dearly. What a great way to be welcomed home. After sex, I gave her a big shopping bag with a bunch of gifts I bought for her on my trip. The assorted goodies consisted of a few outfits I purchased while in Beverly Hills. I also got her a beautiful leather jacket and a necklace worth $5,000. She was happy. I always tried to show her how much I loved her whenever I had the chance.

My father was woken up by the commotion. When he saw me, the disappointment of me coming home was all over his face. It was the quietest month he had had in years. He was now well aware just how deeply involved in drug dealing I was. It must have been awful to have to admit to himself that his once scholarly and athletic son was now a dangerous criminal. The worst part was that he was powerless to do anything about it. My dad had already seen enough shit out of my friends and me to last him a lifetime.

It was only two years earlier that a woman he was dating pulled some real sneaky shit. He met her while he was working as a bouncer at a club called Cooney's. Unbeknownst to him, she had quite the cocaine habit that she kept secret from him. It turns out she was buying the coke off of my sister, who was stealing it from me. At some point, she became tired of paying for it and hatched a devious scheme. This bitch told my father I was dealing coke and warned him that he would get in trouble if the cops ever came into the house. Thanks to my sister's big mouth, she knew where I kept my product. One night when I was out, she persuaded my father to go into my room and get rid of it. As he took the big bag of cocaine from my drawer, she told him not to flush it because the police could find the residue in the toilet. Instead, she convinced him to let her take the coke back to her house so she could discard it. My old man fell for it and gave it to her. She stole what amounted to be about a quarter pound of pure cocaine. This bitch actually had the nerve to brag to people that she had partied on it for months. Once my dad found out what she did, he cut her loose. Just another example of the shit people would do when it comes to drugs, especially cocaine. People were capable of anything and everything.

Days after I returned home, Jake and I figured it was a good time to meet up and discuss the overall situation. There was never any talking on the phone. We assumed the phones were tapped after Kilstein getting busted and Todd dying of an overdose. Not taking any chances, we met way out east at the gun shooting range in Calverton. It was a deep sand pit that was very loud, so the gunfire would drown out our conversation. The first thing I told him left him in disbelief. While I was away, I found out that Ira Kilstein was back in the saddle—slinging product. This was almost impossible to comprehend. It was less than two months since the Feds arrested him for a felony for selling a large amount of cocaine. The only reason Ira would risk doing that was if he was now a DEA informant. If you were cooperating with them, they would definitely let you operate as long as you were handing them bigger fish. That was one of the ways the Feds did things.

Both Jake and I decided to start hustling again anyway. During my vacation, I contemplated switching from the coke to the pot business. My reefer business was growing, so I gave it some thought. There was enough money being made with it to where I could live comfortably. Cocaine sales netted the most cash, but there was a lot less jail time if you were caught hustling marijuana. Jake took a trip into Jackson Heights the next day and picked up four kilos of blow. He took two, and I took two. I figured I would hustle coke a little while longer before transitioning to the weed business for good. We were back rolling again overnight. There was still a lot of heat around, so we really had to be extra careful.

I kept the majority of drugs at a safe house and made deliveries to keep the traffic at my dad's to a minimum. This worked out pretty well for the time being. If the cops wanted to catch me, they would have to nail me going from Point A to Point B. I'd have someone page me from a pay phone, and then I would run to another pay phone to call them back for their order. This really kept the police chasing shadows. There were no cell phones yet, so this was the only safe option.

Now, more than ever, we needed to keep our customers in line. Any one of them who might be dumb enough to stray, and cop off Kilstein while dealing with us, could sink our entire operation. Jake had some monstrous tabs owed to him by a number of people. He found out that one client of his named Joey Toth was sneaking behind his back and going to Kilstein while he was into Jake for twenty grand. Jake was livid. This fucking backstabbing scumbag was not only disrespecting Jake, but he was also putting all of us in jeopardy by doing what he was doing. Time had come to lay down the fucking law.

Driving south on Route 110 in Huntington, Jake and I were on the prowl one afternoon. We were like two lions stalking on the Serengeti. When we passed the light at Schwab Road, I noticed Joey Toth going into Twin Oaks Beverage Distributors. Jake whipped a quick U-turn, we parked right next to Toth's car, got out, and waited. After about five minutes, Joey Toth and one of his boys came walking outside. The both of them were all smiles when they came out the door. That wise ass smirk of Joey's turned into a look of sheer terror once he spotted Jake and me leaning on his car. He knew his number was up. Joey was into Jake for $20k and had been ducking Jake while going behind his back to Kilstein's buying product. Joey Toth began begging and pleading to no avail.

Jake drilled Joey with an overhand right and exploded his nose. Jake then spun him around and put him in a headlock. Joey's shirt pulled up, and I began hitting him in his ribs and kidneys with a barrage of left and right hooks. I must have hit him twenty or thirty times, breaking his ribs, and lacerating one of his kidneys. After a minute or two, Jake started strangling Joey and warned him if he didn't pay up, we would be back. With a lacerated kidney, broken ribs, and a broken nose, the message was received loud and clear. Everyone else in town got the message after word spread of Toth's beating. And believe it or not, there were still a few wise asses stupid enough to test us.

I had mentioned earlier that I did some small loan sharking in addition to the hustling we were doing. There was this burger joint owner whom I had known from school and around town. He was a decent guy for the most part, and I believed him to be a straight shooter. Something was going on with his business, so he came to me explaining that he needed an infusion of cash to make some upgrades to the place. He then asked me to borrow some money for a little while. I asked him how much he needed, and he replied, "$30,000." This was an established business, so I told him I would definitely consider it. If I did it, he offered to pay me back $45,000, which was a decent return for what seemed like nothing risky.

Once I thought it over, I decided to do it. The next day, I met him at his store and brought a duffle bag with thirty grand in it. I gave him the cash, shook his hand, and wished him well. This transaction took place back in September. It was now February, and I hadn't heard from the guy so I was wondering what was up. Not long after we laid the wood to Joey Toth, someone approached me and informed me that this burger joint owner was buying coke off of Kilstein. This enraged me. I was not playing games anymore with anyone as far as business went. There was just too much at stake for me to tolerate anyone crossing the line.

I ended up taking my champagne colored Cadillac Seville for a ride to his house to confront him. When he came out of the house, I fucking snapped. I blasted him in the jaw three or four times and then punched him in the ribs a few more times. He fell under his car, so I stopped. Later that night, I found out that I broke his jaw and cheekbone, and he needed to have his jaw wired up. Not even 24 hours later, someone dropped off a shoebox with $45,000 in it. The day before, I never even mentioned the money he owed. He just wanted to be done with me forever. These types of stories only made our reputation that much more fearsome.

It wasn't that long ago that Long Island was once considered a suburban paradise. It was a place where people such as my parents and others dreamed of moving to so they could give their families a better life. It was a place to raise a family without all of the problems that came with living in the big city. For a long time, that seemed possible. But now things were changing. The country was in the grip of a drug epidemic of the likes we had never seen. Thanks to my fellow hoodlums and me, it was only getting worse.

By this point, most of the bad neighborhoods in New York City had been completely overrun by drugs and the dealers and gangs that controlled them. The living conditions in the hood were near indescribable for the people who lived there. Entire buildings were now turned into dope spots. Whole blocks and sections of neighborhoods were overtaken. The police had not a clue as how to handle the dire situation. One incident would ultimately change that.

Around 3:30 A.M. on February 26, 1988, a police officer named Edward Byrne was sitting in his patrol car on 107th and Inwood avenues in South Jamaica, Queens. He was guarding the house of a certain immigrant who had blown the whistle on a bunch of dope dealers in the area. This man's house had already been firebombed twice in retaliation for his attempts to get rid of the pushers.

Officer Byrne was actually alone in his car when another vehicle rolled up beside his. Two men got out, and one of them knocked on the passenger side window of Byrne's patrol car. While the one man distracted Officer Byrne, the other man snuck up on the officer's side and opened fire with a .38 caliber pistol. Byrne was shot in the head a total of five times. He died shortly after being rushed to the hospital. This triggered a massive investigation. Shortly afterward, four suspects were apprehended who were believed to be involved in the shooting. The police would find out that the hit was ordered by a local drug kingpin named Howard "Pappy" Mason who was on Riker's Island awaiting trial on other charges. All parties involved were convicted and received life sentences. This would be the straw that would break the camel's back. It wouldn't be long after this that the strategies in taking down drug dealers would change.

Immediately following Officer Edward Byrne's execution, the hammer would drop. A new unit would be introduced to help combat the cocaine war now underway. It was called TNT, which stood for Tactical Narcotics Team. And it started right in the area where Officer Byrne was killed. What the police would now do is flood a certain area such as South Jamaica with dozens of undercover officers doing buy and busts, and put everyone under surveillance. Then after accumulating enough evidence, they would sweep the entire area, arresting everyone simultaneously. And soon TNT was operating in almost every drug-infested area in the city. However, the police would soon find out that over half the people they locked up would be right back on the street in no time. The cops were fit to be tied. It was somewhat successful, though. But on Long Island, it wasn't as easy for the cops to infiltrate the drug organizations. Things on Long Island weren't done as out in the open as in the city. And this was the reason the wheels of justice spun much more slowly out here.

The time was now right for a little change. Jake decided to buy a house in another town. He wanted to get out of Huntington with all the police activity going on there, so he ended up buying a house in Commack, which was about ten minutes from Huntington. The house was in a different police sector, but yet still close enough to where it was easy to take care of his clients. It was a smart idea considering all that had gone down recently. I also decided to move and ended up relocating on the other side of Huntington. I ended up moving into a nice size apartment that was the bottom level to a high ranch on East 13th Street. The change of scenery was great, and my father really deserved a break.

Jake and I both got back to our regular routines after we settled into our new homes. We met everyday at 12 o'clock in the afternoon with Master Barathy. Following our grueling 3-hour sessions with him each day, we devoted the rest of our time to hustling and making money. It was full steam ahead for the time being. There was a halfway decent stretch where nothing seemed to go wrong. We were again raking in the dough.

By this time, some of my customers had gone away to school. Being the criminals that they were, they immediately saw an opportunity to capitalize on the potential gold mine that awaited them in college. There was an endless supply of customers, which was great, because we had an unlimited supply of drugs. It was the perfect storm. And it didn't take long for my boys who went away to school to set up shop. Once they enrolled and started classes, things took off. Their businesses just erupted to a level they weren't prepared for. I had friends in three different schools in upstate New York who were now supplying a good portion of the drugs on seven or eight campuses. For a while, things were awesome.

My old dealing partner and pal Kip "Scar" Santiago was taking classes at Cortland University. He was one of the guys who was peddling drugs for me. I kept him in a steady supply of cocaine, marijuana, and steroids. The cocaine I was sending him was the purest you could get. He was cutting the shit and doubling and tripling his money. He was also making a killing on the dozens of pounds of pot I was sending him. But people always want to get greedy, which ends up ruining everything. Even though he was making a small fortune, he was spending more than he made. Up there, Kip was the man, and he really loved being the head honcho. Life was a 24-hour a day party for him. School definitely wasn't his first priority. He became careless, and like most people in this line of work, was totally out for himself.

Now, I was nice enough to send a lot of the drugs to Kip on credit, which was not out of the ordinary because I worked with a lot of my friends that way. This would ultimately backfire in my face. During his dealings, he sold to a couple gangbangers from Brooklyn who were hanging around Cortland with some of their buddies who went to school there. They began enticing Santiago, telling him they had connections for better drugs in Brooklyn. What Kip did not know was that the gangbangers were baiting him to rip him off. They told him that they could get him better drugs for much cheaper prices. Drug dealers got ripped off all the time like this, so Kip should have realized if something sounded too good to be true, it probably was. But like a fool, he fell for it. Unfortunately, I would be the one to pay the price.

Somehow, the bangers convinced Kip to meet them down in Brooklyn. The fucking moron then drove all the way to Brooklyn alone, unarmed with $30,000 of my money on him. When Kip arrived in Bedford Stuyvesant, he met the two guys at some house and parked out front. The gangbangers went inside and left Kip outside in his car. They came outside around twenty minutes later with a pound of some good bud to show him. They told him that the rest is inside and to give them the money. Like a fool, he was dumb enough to hand over the $30,000. The two guys walked inside and then walked right out the back door and were never heard from again. That idiot Santiago waited out front for two hours before he finally realized he had been rolled of the cash.

This kind of shit happened all the time to drug dealers who weren't careful. It was a dirty game, and you had to anticipate these kinds of things. As it would turn out, those two guys were members of the infamous Brooklyn street gang, "The Decepticons." Only greedy Santiago was dumb enough to fall for that shit. Kip came back to me with his tail between his legs and informed me of his betrayal. I fucking lost it on him. I wasn't quite sure what to do with him, so I had to think it through. Finally, I decided I would spoon feed him small amounts of shit so he could start working again to pay off his debt. This was yet another example of how cutthroat this business was, and you should never trust anybody, and I mean anybody.

Even though Jake and I were not the biggest drug dealers around, we were an integral part of the machine that was the drug trade. This was big business, and everyone involved played some important role that kept the wheels turning. America was spending over $100 billion a year on getting high. With the cocaine pouring in incessantly, there was plenty of work to go around if you had the balls to do it. Annually, $79.6 billion was being spent on cocaine, $21.8 billion was spent on heroin. Over 11 billion dollars' worth of marijuana was being sold a year. And more than $5 billion was being spent on other assorted illegal drugs, such as methamphetamine and pills. The numbers were mind-boggling. The Medellin Cartel in Colombia grossed over $5 billion in 1988 alone. It broke down basically like this: The Cartel would ship large shipments of drugs into the United States, to places like New York, Chicago, and Los Angeles, where the biggest consumer markets were. Then the brokers would break down those loads to sell to big dealers, who would then start supplying distributors who hooked up dealers like Jake and me. After that, we would sell to smaller dealers who would then start hooking up the street dealers. Last but not least, it would reach the consumer, who was the most vital piece of the puzzle. Without them, there would be no cash being spent on the product. It essentially came down to supply and demand. There was a never-ending appetite for illegal drugs, and America was by far the hungriest.

Around this time, Jake would make some decisions that would ultimately seal his fate. He was now living in a very nice two-story house in Commack and was enjoying his new surroundings. The house was a high ranch that was painted white and had a good size backyard. Jake had a safe installed into the cement floor in the basement. Where the garage was, now held a small apartment. Thanks to his business, people were coming by day and night for their cocaine. It was like a 7-11 store in the middle of this fairly ritzy neighborhood. The first bad move came when Jake offered the apartment to this guy named Maurice Taramina. Maurice was a former brown belt in the American Combat Karate system. He was originally from Levittown. What stood out most to me is how shady the guy was. When you shook his hand, it felt like you were shaking a wet sponge. I didn't trust him one bit. Jake, on the other hand, looked up to him, and I couldn't understand why. This would be a costly mistake.

Maurice moved in right away and began scoping out the scene. Maurice definitely took notice. He began hitting Jake up for free drugs and cash every day. I warned Jake about my gut feeling with the guy, and of course, he wouldn't listen. This would become a recurring theme. For some reason, I had this terrible feeling about Maurice, and it would prove to be prophetic. I could see something bad coming with this scumbag but wasn't sure what or when it would happen. Jake treated this guy like a king, and it would soon blow up in his face. Remember what I said about trusting no one.

Maurice ended up being a total leach and was good for nothing. He didn't work and paid no rent at all. It made no sense him being there around all of our wheeling and dealing. But Jake had to keep him around, despite all the warning signs. This guy Maurice was jealous over everything Jake and I had going on. He was envious over the fact that we were making money and were also training with Master Barathy, five days a week. He was also witnessing how Jake ran his entire operation. I don't think Jake realized how dangerous it was what he was doing. In this lifestyle, there is no such thing as loyalty no matter how much you want to believe it. And there would be no loyalty from Maurice, no matter how much Jake did for him.

One Thursday afternoon, I answered the phone to find out Jake had scored four tickets to see the Rolling Stones at Shea Stadium on their Steel Wheel's Tour. He asked me if I wanted to go, and I said, "Hell yeah." The concert was the next evening. Accompanying us would be my buddy Jobo and Master Richie Barathy, our karate instructor. We were all really excited to go.

After a great night's sleep, I awoke with a smile, knowing in only hours, I was going to be second row to see Mick Jagger and the Rolling Stones. Jake was the one who would drive us all there. For the show, we had weed, cocaine, and Percodan. Around 7 o'clock that night, Jake left his house to pick us up. Just as he was leaving, that scrum bag Maurice was standing on the front lawn of Jake's house with this phony smile on his face and said, "Enjoy the show." Jake didn't think anything of it at the time but later admitted that something was wrong with Maurice's demeanor.

Once Jake picked all of us up, we drove about thirty minutes into Queens to Shea Stadium. We got hammered on the way. When we got to our seats, we were thrilled at how close we were to the stage. An hour later, the lights went down. As the curtains came down, Jake panicked and ran to the port-o-potty and locked himself in. He had a really bad anxiety attack from the pot we smoked. The other three of us stayed in our seats and were treated to one of the best shows I had ever seen. Mick Jagger was amazing.

The show lasted three hours, and the Stones finished up with Honky-Tonk Women, where these 50-foot blow up dolls popped up on both sides of the stage. What a dynamite concert the Rolling Stones put on. Jake met us back at the car when it was over. Master Barathy, Jobo, and I were all wrecked and had some trouble finding our way back to the car. Jake was still all kinds of fucked up from smoking that weed. We made it back to Huntington fairly late. After Jake dropped me off, I headed inside and began unwinding. Twenty minutes later, the phone rang.

It was Jake, and he could barely speak. He asked me to come over and told me that it was urgent. I hung up the phone, hopped into my car, and raced over to his house in Commack. When I ran inside, Jake yelled for me to come downstairs into the basement. When I opened the basement door, I was stunned. There was a giant cloud of dust that nearly suffocated me. I then put my shirt over my mouth and nose, headed down the stairs, and noticed Jake sitting on the bench press sobbing uncontrollably. I then looked over and noticed a hole in the cement floor where his safe used to be. The hole was about two feet by two feet. All Jake could say was that he had been robbed. And Maurice was nowhere to be found. It was pretty easy to see now what happened.

That fucking scumbag Maurice waited for the perfect time to strike. He hired a few thugs he knew from Nassau County, and as soon as Jake left for the show, they came in and jackhammered the safe out of the floor. It was that simple. I asked Jake what they got, and he again broke down when he told me. They got him for a quarter million in cash, over a kilo of cocaine, ten thousand morphine and Xanax pills, and also took four of his guns. Two of the guns were assault rifles. Jake was completely devastated. I couldn't blame him because I would have been the same way had it happened to me. I hate to say it, but I saw this coming when he let that piece of shit move in. Again, I can't stress enough how you can't trust anyone in this damn business. To make things worse, Jake couldn't call the police. What would he tell them, that someone stole his cocaine and pills and a stash of cash he made illegally? Of course not, he would have to handle this himself.

But first, Jake needed to start hustling again so he could make some of his money back. He was temporarily broke except for the money he had on the street that he now needed to collect. He asked for my help, and I was happy to do so because he was my boy. Instead of sweating the customers who owed him cash, I ended up loaning him the money so he could pick up a couple of kilos of blow to get his business up and running again. Things started moving along pretty quickly because he already had the established clientele, so that wasn't a problem. The only real problem now was what to do about that Maurice scumbag who robbed Jake. Jake put some feelers out, and within a week some news started to get back to him.

After pulling off the robbery, Maurice supposedly had to split the cash and drugs up four ways with the crew who did it with him. He then began renting hotel rooms and smoking up all the cocaine he had made off with. Maurice had the balls to rip Jake off, but now he feared for his life. And for good reason, Jake was going to kill him on site. When Maurice would take a hit of freebase, he would grab the AR-15 he stole and start bugging out, totally panic stricken. He knew he was a marked man.

Soon after gathering some intel, Jake rounded up a dozen guys all armed to the teeth and began to hunt him down. They got word that Maurice was shacking up with some crack whore smoking up every night. Believing they had found the right house, the boys surrounded the place. At the same time, Jake kicked in the front door while another guy kicked in the back door. Jake grabbed the three or four crack heads inside, and they couldn't rat out Maurice fast enough. Maurice had just left the house twenty minutes earlier.

Angry about just missing him, Jake and the boys' next stop was a crack motel Maurice had been hiding out in. All the local junkies frequented the spot. Maurice was staying in Room 116. Without hesitation, Jake kicked the door down and saw one of Maurice's buddies lying on the bed. Again, they just missed him. So out of frustration, they beat this junkie within an inch of his life. Jake knocked out most of the guy's teeth when he hit him in the mouth with the butt of a 12-gauge Mossberg shotgun. The boys jumped in and just beat the living daylights out of him. The man sustained a broken jaw, two black eyes, a broken nose, a broken arm, and had his ribs broken. Jake clearly was sending Maurice a message that when he did catch him, he was finished. And word of Maurice's friend's beating spread quickly. Once Maurice found out about what happened to his good buddy at the motel, he ran like a scared rabbit. I mean he literally vanished. There were rumors that he left the state, and some people told us he was so afraid that he tried going to the police. Whatever the case was, the trail went cold from that point on. So it was now time again to focus on business.

The following week, I had a real close call in almost getting busted. On a gorgeous afternoon, I was out in Commack taking a guitar lesson, which I did every other week. Normally I paid my teacher cash for them, which is how I had always done it to that point. A few weeks earlier, my guitar teacher asked me if I could front him an ounce of cocaine and let him work it off. I never told him I was a dealer, but he found out through my neighbor about my occupation. I told him I would do it for him, only I didn't say when. So that day I brought it with me to give to him. My idea was to surprise him when the lesson was over. The lesson was difficult, and I ended up forgetting to give it to him. When I pulled out of his driveway to head home, I was completely unaware that I had twenty-eight grams of cocaine in my guitar case. Big mistake.

I got on the Northern State Parkway where it begins on Veteran's Highway and started driving west toward Huntington. The sun was shining bright, and

I turned on Van Halen One and began to accelerate faster in my beautiful Mustang GT. In that car, it was very easy to surpass the speed limit without realizing it. Between that and the music blasting, I lost track of what was going on and wasn't paying attention to the fact that I was doing 80 mph in a 55 mph zone.

After a few minutes, a song called "I'm the One" came on, and I almost fell into a trance. It was a rip-roaring, swinging rock and roll song by Van Halen that always got me amped up whenever I heard it. I came up to a left curve in the roadway, and suddenly, there were these real big bushes obstructing my view of an old gas station that was closed down years earlier but was still standing. The problem was that sometimes, state troopers would sit there and bust people for speeding.

Well, today wasn't going to be my lucky day. As I passed the bushes, I spotted one of those brownish gray state trooper patrol cars sitting at the old gas station. Glancing down, I noticed I was doing 85 mph. I was really moving. When I was passing him, I tried hitting the brakes, but it was too late. His lights went on, and he immediately began pursuit to pull me over. Not knowing why I said, "Fuck it," and hit the gas. My speed increased to over 120 mph, and he became a distant blip in my rear view mirror. Thinking I was home free, I couldn't believe it when I got caught behind two full lanes of traffic that I was unable to navigate around.

Seconds later, he was right up my ass. A quick decision had to be made, and it was a bad one. I saw that the Deer Park Avenue exit was coming up on my right. Acting like I was going to pass it, I decided to make the turn, hoping he wouldn't be able to turn off that quickly. Well, I was wrong. When I turned off, my rear wheel caught the curb and spun my car 180 degrees. Just as my car turned around, I looked and saw the state trooper with his hands up, covering his face, bracing for impact. We hit each other head on, doing about 60 mph. In that split second, I remembered I had the cocaine in the guitar case. My car stalled after the collision, and it wouldn't start. I said, "Holy shit," and realized I was going to be in huge trouble if they found this. I needed to get rid of the coke.

Instinctively, I grabbed the cocaine and made a mad dash for it. I knew I wasn't going to get away; I just needed to get far enough away to stash the shit. My heart was pounding. The trooper couldn't believe it when he saw me bolt on foot. With white smoke billowing from under his hood, he threw his wrecked car in drive, and the chase was on. He was right up my ass, so I began to zig zag down the street. I tried running over people's lawns, but he followed closely, mowing down bushes on the front lawns while chasing me. I made it about 300 yards to the fire house on Deer Park Avenue and hopped a six foot fence. Seeing a tree with a hole in it, I wasted no time in disposing of the product. Now completely winded, I stopped to catch my breath. As I did, some farmer yelled, "He's over here, Officer." When I turned around, the state trooper was standing there pointing his .38 caliber revolver at me. The trooper screamed, "Get on the ground," and I did just that. Luckily, I was able to get rid of the blow, which was my only concern. The trooper knocked me around pretty hard while cuffing me. I only spent a night in jail, which was nothing considering what might have been had he found the cocaine. My ordeal wouldn't go unnoticed.

The next day, a friend of mine called to tell me that I had made the paper. It was an article in Newsday titled, "Chase Ends in Crash." Everyone I knew saw it. My buddies laughed about that for months. They thought that I was insane. I must have been for pulling a stunt like that. My parents, on the other hand, weren't as amused. My mother was mortified when she found out about it after reading the paper. She called me and voiced her displeasure. It didn't shock her because I had many run-ins with the police prior to this. In the end, I walked away with a slap on the wrist. After wrecking a state police car during a chase that exceeded 120 mph, I only had to pay a $500 fine. The District Attorney recommended six months in jail, but my lawyer convinced the judge to give me a fine.

Jake and I once again focused our efforts on business, and business meant slinging product. Both of us would soon discover that our girlfriends were up to no good. His girl and my girl were both partiers when we met them, so this would come as no surprise. For a while, Vanessa and Jake's girl Tina were doing well, but eventually every good thing comes to an end. You could chalk it up to karma. While training hard with the karate, we took some serious lumps. Following a particularly rough week training maybe a year earlier, I tried some Percodan, which is an extremely effective opioid painkiller. I could not believe how good they were. Not only did they kill my pain, they also got me high as a kite. I loved them.

So, fast-forward a year to the present. Vanessa had gotten into a car accident. Nothing too bad, but she was in some pain. I then did something I would regret forever. I offered her a couple of Percodan, not realizing the potential trouble this would later bring about. She took them, and maybe fifteen or twenty minutes later I saw her eyes light up. Yes sir, they had definitely rang her bells. She was now pain free and was just as high as I was the year before when I tried them for the first time. I only took them once in a while because I was extremely disciplined and knew I could get out of control very easily if I started taking them regularly. But Vanessa only knew one speed, and that was full throttle. She immediately began pestering me for them, and I could see this was going to be a problem.

Unfortunately, the genie was now out of the bottle, and there was no way to get her back in. Jake's girlfriend Tina started using cocaine again, and that drove him nuts. He didn't use drugs and didn't approve of his girl doing them either. In reality, neither Jake nor I had any control of their drug use even though we thought we did. So the train started to come off the tracks. Jake and I were both in way over our heads. Both Vanessa and Tina would give us more than either one of us could handle. And in reality, it probably served us right for the sins we were committing.

Jake's girl started stealing from him, and my girl did the same to me. It was not only drugs, but also cash. Even though the two girls never hung out, they started doing a lot of the same things. They started going out to clubs again and were doing things they knew really pissed us off. And let's not even talk of the affairs they had behind our backs. Though both were treated like queens, neither one showed any loyalty or appreciation for anything that was done for them. In hindsight, we should have expected nothing less. Shit, they were cocaine queens when we met them. To make matters worse, Vanessa also started with the cocaine again. This situation was getting out of control. When it came down to it, there is no way to talk someone out of using drugs. That's the bottom line.

Despite the problems going on with the girls, somehow we still managed to continue our operation. Believe me, it wasn't easy. It's very dangerous when you have people that close to you who are heading off of a cliff and could easily take you with them. We really had to be careful. Maybe it was the distraction of his girlfriend that had caused Jake to make the terrible decision of letting Maurice move in, but, unfortunately, it wouldn't be the last of his bad decisions. His next few would seal the deal.

It would be a knock at the door that would ignite a flurry of activity, which would ultimately impact our lives in the near and not so distant future. That knock would come to Jake's door on a night that we were in his living room, watching a ball game, and practicing martial art technique. Jake casually strolled over to answer the door and was surprised when he opened it. There, standing at the door, was Chris Campanella, and the late Todd O'Connor's brother, Scott. As I mentioned earlier in the book, Chris was a member of the infamous Crash and Carry Gang. The Crash and Carry Gang was a band of thieves whom had a unique style of robbery. They would smash a window of a high-end store that usually carried extremely expensive merchandise. Then they would go in and grab as many items as they could before making their getaway. And the gang had nearly perfected this style of crime. They were responsible for hundreds of robberies in New York City and Long Island.

Upon entering Jake's house, we all exchanged greetings. It had been nearly a year since we had seen each other, so we were a little surprised they had just popped over out of nowhere. As it turns out, they had been busy, and I mean extremely busy. And when I said busy, I also meant naughty. The gang had pulled dozens of jobs in the past year. This ended up being the reason for the visit from them. They had loads and loads of merchandise they were looking to unload. They had hit a bunch of fur stores on the Upper East Side of Manhattan that sold really luxurious coats such as mink, silver fox, Russian sable, and chinchilla. The coats had price tags that sold from anywhere from $5,000 to $25,000 apiece. The gang also had hit some expensive men's boutiques and jewelry stores.

Jindo Furs and Antonovich Furs were just two of many that fell victim to them. Jindo Furs was located on Third Avenue and 60th Street. In the newspapers, it was described something like this. "It was like a bomb hit the store," said the Vice President of Jindo Furs. "They drove a truck right through the window and knocked down an inner gate we had put up inside of the window. They then took about 75–80 furs and drove off."

In order to buy themselves extra time to do the job, they would set up a diversion. So before the gang hit these places, they would synchronize their watches, and five to ten minutes before they would do the robbery, they would have one of their buddies who was all the way across town either break a jewelry store window, or make some bogus 911 call to the police to lure them away from the actual crime scene. It was brilliant. And to this point, it worked like a charm. Millions of dollars worth of merchandise was stolen in a very short period of time.

Right after these scores, they would stash the goods at warehouses or safe houses until things cooled off a bit before moving them. And that time was now. Chris asked Jake if he could help fence some of these items. I personally wasn't crazy about the idea when hearing about this, but Jake with a big smile on his face said, "Okay." The reason I thought this wasn't the smartest idea was that the FBI was all over these guys by now. Being a drug dealer, the last thing you need is to get caught up accidentally in someone else's trouble, especially by a law enforcement agency as capable as the FBI. But bad decisions were becoming routine for Jake by now, so to me, it wasn't surprising. And it wasn't just the Crash and Carry Gang being eyeballed by the Feds. One of my weed connections, Charlie Sykes, had the DEA breathing down his neck hard. His tanning salon in Massapequa that he owned was busted getting a UPS delivery with 100 pounds of marijuana in it. He also had a truckload of over 800 pounds that was busted in New Mexico. Sykes was really starting to feel the heat.

The next week or so passed rather quickly. Then I got a call from Jake, who told me to come over and bring plenty of money. I said, "What the hell?" and drove over to his house, which usually took me about twenty minutes. There was a good size truck out front. My mind started spinning with curiosity. As Jake opened the front door, he had this shit-eating grin on his face that caught my attention. It was his up to no good face. I followed him to the basement door, and we proceeded to go downstairs. Like one of the other times I went down those stairs, I was again in for a major surprise.

When I got to the bottom, I looked around and was blown away. I couldn't believe what I was seeing. They had rigged these poles hanging horizontally from the ceiling, and hanging from them were hundreds of magnificent fur coats. They were all breathtaking. Chris Campanella was darting back and forth arranging them as best he could. Some of the furs were the ones stolen from those Manhattan outlets. They ranged in sizes from short to medium to full length. And they were all top of the line. Chris then turned to me and gave me a big hug and said, "Pat, I'm going to take real good care of you." He told me to look at everything and to take my time. He said he wanted me to have the first pick of the merchandise. I was sure as shit happy about that.

When I saw something I liked, Chris would pull it down like a salesman at a store would do and helped me put it on. It was absolutely hilarious. There was over a million dollars worth of furs hanging up down there. I picked out four of them, two for me, and two for my girl. I ended up taking one full-length mink and one three-quarter length mink. I also grabbed a full-length silver fox coat and a three-quarter length silver fox coat. They were stunning to say the least. The only thing more stunning than the way they looked was the price of them. Chris gave them to me for $500 a piece. All four cost well over $5,000 with the two minks costing more than $10,000 each. After I was done shopping, they opened the place up to everyone else. Jake called everyone he knew and told them to come over. Within the hour, there were at least twenty people there all shopping like they were in an actual store. The place was a madhouse. You would have to have been there to see what it was like.

Jake's house was in your typical middle class neighborhood in Commack. And now, it looked like it was Macy's Department Store during a one-day sale. I stayed for about another hour before leaving with my goods. But while I was there, I witnessed people come in, shop, and walk out the door with these fur coats worth thousands of dollars. The neighbors must have been baffled with what they were seeing. The funny thing was that the whole time that this was going on, and it was going on all day, the FBI had not a clue as to what was happening. They were losing their minds trying to figure it out.

After the one-day blow out sale, Chris packed up the truck, which was stolen by the way, with the remaining furs and took off. But this would not be the last we would see of him. For a while, this actually became a pretty regular thing. During that one day, Jake had over fifty people come to his house. He was really taking a huge risk considering that he was also selling cocaine from the same residence. This couldn't continue, could it? Well, it sure as hell did. It actually became comical. None of us really cared too much about consequences at that time. We were all in our early 20s then and were fearless for the most part. We were living like a bunch of modern day outlaws and were all only getting started in our budding criminal careers.

The next weekend, the circus continued. This time, however, the merchandise would be expensive men's wear. So after getting up Saturday morning, I again received a call from my training partner Jake. When he told me to come over, it wasn't hard to piece together as to why. His tone gave it away. Entering Jake's house, I could hear the song "Long Time" by the rock band Boston blasting on the stereo. Unlike the week before, I kind of knew what to expect this time. Before I even opened the basement door, I broke down laughing uncontrollably. Jake stopped and asked me, "What's so funny?" I was laughing so hard I couldn't even tell him why so I motioned for him to go downstairs.

I followed him down just like the week before, and even though I knew what to expect, it still surprised me. Once again, hanging from the ceiling, was a huge amount of stolen merchandise. This time, there were hundreds of men's suits. There were also some fancy leather jackets and some long raincoats. Again, all of it was top of the line. Designers, such as Georgio Armani and Canali, made the suits. The prices of the Italian suits ranged between $500 and $2,500 apiece. The leather jackets and raincoats were also really expensive. These were the types of clothes you would see on investment bankers or Wall Street tycoons. They were stolen from some upscale men's boutiques in Manhattan and Nassau County earlier that year.

At the time we weren't sure where it all came from, but honestly, we really didn't care and didn't ask questions. All I knew was that I was getting a great deal, and that was all that mattered. I once again saw Chris Campanella setting everything up, trying to get it ready for the onslaught of customers who were about to start flocking to Jake's house for a once in a lifetime type of deal. It was the perfect hustle. Chris needed customers to unload the stolen merchandise he had, and Jake who was already established as a dealer, knew dozens of other drug dealers who were all flush with cash. It worked out perfectly.

Thanks to Chris, I again got first crack at what merchandise I wanted and took full advantage of it. Chris totally hooked me up. I bought five beautiful suits that were just my size. I also grabbed two leather jackets and two long raincoats. In all, I got about $12,000 worth of stuff for $2,500. After I paid Chris, I went outside and put it all in my Cadillac Seville. This time, I decided to hang around for the afternoon. It was really something to see. With the rock music blasting inside the house, car after car after car began pulling up and people began heading into Jake's. Chris was playing tailor while trying to help all the customers into their desired size and fit in the clothing. The scene was quite amusing. It was a smooth operation overall and lasted most of the day, wrapping up around 7 P.M.

I laid low for the next week and then decided to meet up with Jake to discuss some business. With all the recent activity going on at his house, we ended up meeting up at the Eastern Athletic Club on Jericho Turnpike in Huntington. This was a regular spot of ours. The Eastern Athletic Club had very good weight training equipment and a bunch of tennis and racquetball courts. We went there at least a few times a week to lift weights and play racquetball. The racquetball helped us with cardio, which ultimately benefitted us in the martial arts.

That afternoon after meeting there, we hit the weights for a good hour. Then we began a fierce hour of racquetball. This is where we did our talking because the courts were enclosed. Jake told me he was making another run into Jackson Heights to pick up a load. He would be picking up four kilos of cocaine and something extra this time. Jake explained to me that the coke connection also had a nice size amount of Thai stick marijuana, sixty pounds of it. If I wanted in on it, I had to let him know and had to give him the cash that evening before he left. I said, "Fuck yeah," I wanted in. During our game, we planned to meet up at my father's house. Now, dripping sweat from the racquetball game, we took a sauna and showered before leaving.

We met at my Dad's at 7 P.M. I gave Jake $60,000, and he had another $60,000 of his own money. When he was leaving, I told him to watch his back. He had over 100 grand in the trunk of his car, so he would be prime-pickings if someone wanted to roll him for the cash. Jake was packing a Colt 9mm just in case. The connect we had in the city was legit so he really wasn't worried about them pulling anything. The police, on the other hand, weren't nearly as trustworthy. Corruption in the New York City Police Department was at an all-time high. Cops would think nothing of pulling someone over and robbing some drug dealer for his cash. It happened all the time. You see there was so much money in circulation due to the drug trade that everyone wanted a taste. Even cops. Lucky for us, Jake made the trip without any problems. Around midnight, we met back at my Dad's to split up the load. I took a kilo of coke and forty pounds of the pot. The weed was awesome. It was Thai stick, which back in the 1980s was considered really quality smoke. Sad to say, it would be the last Thai stick seen in the United States from there on out.

What ended up happening was a ship called the Encounter Bay, which was an oil freighter, was stopped by the Coast Guard somewhere off the coast of Washington State in June 1988. Aboard it, the authorities found 72 tons of Southeast Asian Thai stick. It may have been the largest marijuana seizure to that point. The Feds linked the load to a New York man named Brian Daniels, who had been living in Thailand for years and was the biggest pot dealer in the world. They eventually caught up to Daniels in Switzerland and arrested him. The courts came down hard on him when he was sentenced. Daniels got 25 years plus 25 years. His arrest essentially shut down the flow of Thai stick to the U.S. forever.

The load we got turned over immediately. I shipped all the pot upstate to my clients at school along with half of the cocaine. The rest I sold locally.

Things were again moving pretty smoothly, which was always a good thing. But soon enough, something would come along to fuck things up. And that thing that would do it would be an old dreaded face, which I had hoped would never come back around. Sometime during that next week, while Jake was in Huntington, he ran into Ira Kilstein. Kilstein was the dealer in town, who a year and a half earlier almost got me busted when he sold nine ounces of cocaine to a DEA informant.

I don't know why, but Jake actually talked to him and made arrangements to hang out with him. He must have been out of his fucking mind to do that. When I found out, I flipped out. I told Jake he was playing with fire. For the past two years, we had been avoiding Kilstein like the plague. For some stupid reason, Jake found the idea of getting together with Kilstein entertaining.

Well, this would be the costliest decision of all for Jake. There had been too many close calls to risk getting involved with Ira Kilstein on any level. I wanted no part of it at all and told Jake so. My reason being was that two years earlier Kilstein was busted selling major weight in cocaine to the DEA and never did a day in jail. He started dealing again right away, and his business was now booming. How was this possible? I could think of a few reasons, and they were all bad. I reminded Jake of that, but it fell on deaf ears. This is around the time I tried to separate myself from being caught up with that foolish nonsense. It was hard to do because Jake was my best buddy and training partner in karate, so we still saw each other at our lessons.

Initially, Kilstein's and Jake's involvement with each other seemed like no big deal, but I knew better. I knew this was going to end badly one way or the other. I just made sure I wasn't around when they hung out. Kilstein had become so flamboyant or ostentatious it was disturbing. He had by now accumulated quite a bit of luxury items that consisted of a Mercedes Benz, a BMW, a $100,000 Mustang that he raced out east, and a Scarab racing boat worth over $100,000. For someone who was busted two years earlier, he was doing his best to show everyone that he was in business and not even remotely worried about law enforcement. That was the troubling part to me because I always tried to remain low key in my business affairs. Flaunting it and taunting the police was not smart. Jake, on the other hand, didn't seem to be bothered by all of the showboating Kilstein was doing. Jake would eventually regret the decision he made, just not yet. It would take some time to finally see the light. The only real question was just what it was going to cost him. And it wouldn't be long in finding out. I'll tell you more about it, but I'm going to change gears for a minute.

After a few routine and uneventful weeks had passed, we received some exciting news. We got it at our karate lesson. Jake and I waited patiently as Master Barathy entered the karate school. He came in with this big smile on his face and gave both of us the American Combat handshake. We bowed as a sign of respect, which is what we always did whenever we saw him. Barathy got right to it. He told us he got a call from his buddy George Goldsmith, who was a screenwriter in Hollywood. Goldsmith offered Master Barathy a part in some movie that was about to start filming right away. Master Barathy agreed to take it, and asked the Director Bill Milling if he would use Jake and me in the fight scene. The Director said it was okay. Everything was now set. We were ecstatic. It may not have been a big deal to Master Barathy, but to Jake and me, this was huge.

Master Barathy had the look of a big-time movie star. He was 6 feet tall on a chiseled 190-pound frame. He had really long, jet black hair and a dark complexion. His most unique feature were the twin combat dragon tattoos on his forearms. The part of the film we were going to be in was going to be filmed in the Bahamas.

When we arrived in the Bahamas, it was stifling hot, around 100 degrees. We took a cab to a resort called the Crystal Palace that was right on the water. This is where we all would stay. The movie was being shot all around the resort and in the water on a pirate ship. Master Barathy had arrived three days earlier because he was in other scenes in the film that were being filmed before we got there. Jake and I brought our girls with us so they could take a vacation while we were working. The first day, we hung around the resort and waited for Master Barathy to come back from a long day of filming. He had spent most of the day filming in the casino. Master Barathy was delighted to see us.

It was now nighttime, and there was a huge party going on in the back of the resort. It was mostly members of the film crew, the movie stars, and their families. Jake and I followed Master Barathy as he led the way down to the party. He began introducing us to anyone who was of any importance. We met Director Bill Milling first. Next, we were introduced to most of the stars from the movie. It featured Frank Gorshin, who played the Riddler in the TV show "Batman." He was a cool guy, and I had a few drinks with him. We were then introduced to Pricilla Barnes, James Hong, and Dick Van Patten. Each had fairly successful careers in Hollywood. That night we all got tuned up pretty good. Master Barathy and I chewed some Percodan as we continued to get hammered. I managed to smuggle in some weed from back home, which Master Barathy appreciated. We partied until 3 am.

We had to be up at 6 A.M., so when I received my wake up call, I was hung over pretty bad. Being so young, I thankfully was able to shake off my hangover and get moving. By 7 A.M., we were shuttled out to this old-fashioned pirate ship, which sat about 500 yards off shore. The scene we were supposed to shoot ended up being delayed for two days. That's Hollywood for you. What really sucked was that Jake and I had to spend those next few days in a cabin under the deck of the ship, waiting until they were ready for our scene to be filmed. By day three, we finally got our chance to work in front of the camera. In the blazing sun, the crew set up for what was supposed to be our fight scene.

It started out like a disaster. The director said to just improvise on the spot, which made no sense to me at all. We tried it anyway. I heard the director say, "Ready and Action." We went through the motions for about a minute before the director yelled, "Cut." He then screamed out that it was awful. I went to Master Barathy with an idea. He then grabbed the director and asked him if we could have ten minutes while he and I choreographed a short fight scene. The director, Bill Milling, obliged. In only five minutes, we came up with a great little scene. We explained to the other stunt guys exactly what we wanted, and they were ready. Now came the moment of truth. Again, the director yelled, "Ready and Action." It was hard to believe, but we nailed it in two takes. The director was finally happy with what we did, and he thanked us. It took nearly two hours to film what would end up being a two-minute scene in the movie. In the end, it was worth it. Jake and I were now in a movie fighting with our instructor. The movie's name was "Joker's Wild," and it ended up going straight to home video and TV. The remainder of our time in the Bahamas was spent eating out and gambling in the casino. The five days flew by and before you knew it, we were leaving to go back to New York and reality. Only this time, the stakes would be raised drastically.

It was now 1990, and it would prove to be a year with historic significance. On August 2, Suddam Hussein and his Iraqi army would invade the small country of Kuwait. It was viewed as a major act of aggression by the United

States and other free world nations. This would prompt a quick response by allied forces, and a massive build up of troops began in the desert in what was known as Operation Desert Shield. The United States was leading the charge of what would be the largest military action since the Vietnam War ended April 30, 1975. This ultimately led to war thousands of miles from our homeland. As that was happening, there was another war going on at home. The war on drugs, and make no mistake about it, it was destroying this country from within. People were dying every day. My boys and I were on the front lines for it, and it seemed to be getting worse as each day passed.

When our plane landed back in New York City after our trip, the place was like a powder keg ready to explode. Mayor David Dinkins was only in office a little while, but had the unfortunate luck of having started his term during what would be New York City's most violent year on record. By the end of 1990, there would be 2,245 murders. And a lot of them were drug related.

Every day you could read the newspapers and see one horror story after another that all had a similar scene, drugs. No community was immune to the problem, because it was everywhere. Rich and poor alike were all affected in some way by it, and it was usually bad. A movie that had just come out did a great job of capturing the vibe of the drug trade at that time. It starred Christopher Walken and was called the "King of New York." Although it was fiction, it really nailed it. Drugs, violence, and greed were the main story lines, and most of all it showed you how cutthroat this business was.

After getting settled in following our Bahamas trip, we hit the ground running. Jake took the usual trip into Jackson Heights, Queens, to pick up our cocaine. He returned with another three or four kilos that we split up. Jake was moving more coke than I was, so he took the bigger amount. The next day when I went to pick it up, something strange happened. When he gave me my package, we were about to go outside as a cop car pulled up right in front of his house. Thirty seconds later, another one pulled up. Then two minutes later, another three cop cars rolled up. Jesus, this did not look good. To our delight, the cops got out of their cars and went to the house across the street. It ended up being some kind of domestic dispute. We left the cocaine in Jake's house and stepped out onto his front lawn to see what was up.

A few minutes later, while Jake and I were talking, Chris Campanella came cruising up in a stolen Mustang. These guys changed stolen cars like they did their underwear. Chris has brass balls. He had the nerve to start beeping at the cops because they were blocking the road. Believe it or not, they actually moved for him. Chris pulled into Jake's driveway, hopped out, and we began chatting. Twenty minutes later, the cops split. Then the real talking started.

Chris and some of the Crash and Carry Gang wanted to make a few quick scores around our area. We gave him some ideas. The first place they would hit would be a pharmacy in Huntington. I knew someone who worked in the pharmacy, so I got them the layout to the store, which showed what cabinets to hit once they got inside. The second place the gang would hit was going to be a P.C. Richard's in Hauppauge. P.C. Richard's sold TVs, stereos, and other expense electronic goods. And the third store would be a sporting goods store in Deer Park.

Less than a week later, the gang knocked off the pharmacy. One of them cut in through the roof and dropped down on to the counter in front of the cabinets. They filled two sizable duffle bags and left. Jake and I met Chris the next day to see what he got from the pharmacy. He had sealed bottles of Percodan and Percocet with a thousand pills in each. There were five of each, totaling 10,000 opiate painkillers. The painkillers were becoming a widely abused drug by now, so we had customers for all of them. Chris also had sealed bottles of Morphine, Vicodin, Dilaudid, Xanax, and Valium. We took them all off his hands.

About a week later, the gang struck again. This time it would be P.C. Richards that went down, and down they went. The gang used that big stolen box truck to do the job. What they did was waited until nighttime for the store to close. Around 10 o'clock, they pulled the truck close enough to the store to observe. Then one of the boys cut the phone line or the alarm line to the store, which triggered the alarm deliberately. Next, they waited for the police to respond to the alarm going off. When the cops showed up, they found nothing wrong except that the alarm was going off. So the police contacted the alarm company and had them turn off the alarm. The police stayed for about an hour until they got a call about a jewelry store across town that was being robbed. One of the gang broke a window to the jewelry store to draw the cops away from P.C. Richard's. Once the cops left, the gang pulled right up to the store, broke in, and cleaned them out.

They filled the entire truck from floor to ceiling with all the highest priced TVs, stereos, and whatever else was inside the store. Quietly, they pulled away when they were finished and stashed everything for a few days until they knew the heat was off. Most of this load they moved themselves, but they did send over enough to Jake's to warrant another blow out sale.

With his basement again full of stolen goodies, Jake dialed as many people as he could and invited them over for some fantastic bargains. As always, I got first dibs and bought myself a big screen TV. I ended up paying very little for a brand new TV and speakers. When I took off, everyone else started coming by. Chris marked all of the merchandise down to a third of their regular prices. Every bit of the stolen loot went in less than a day. Each time they wrapped it up, Chris gave Jake a nice cut for helping fence the goods. We didn't hear from the robbery crew for the next few weeks because we decided to keep a low profile for a little bit. Both Jake and I continued our drug operations, though. We each made a killing off of the pharmaceuticals that were stolen from the pharmacy. Things were about to change drastically for one of us. Someone was about to be permanently removed from the chessboard.

The third and final job that was going to be pulled in the area was sporting goods store on Deer Park Avenue in Deer Park. It carried hundreds of Adidas, Fila, and Sergio Tacchini sweat suits that were very popular at the time. The suits sold for anywhere from $100 - $250 a piece. I know it didn't fit with the high-end jobs the crash and carry gang did, but it seemed to be an easy mark. I remember asking Chris Campanella why he liked stealing so much, and his response was, "I get a rush from it, like a junkie." He said, "If I saw a lacrosse stick in someone's car, I would have to steal it even though it wasn't worth anything." There lies a clue to the mindset of some of these brazen criminals.

Some of the members of the gang went into the sporting goods store to do a recon of the place. They wanted to see the easiest way in and out, and exactly where everything in the store was located. After doing their homework, they came up with a plan. This was going to be in their trademark smash and grab style that they were famous for.

At approximately 11 P.M., four days later after the store was closed, they rammed a van right through the front window. As glass shattered everywhere with the alarm going off, a group of them exited the van rather quickly and entered the store. Knowing where everything they were going to steal was, they began pulling dozens of sweat suits at a time off the rack. Although the alarm was ringing, it didn't phase them in the slightest. They methodically loaded the van with as many suits as they could fit in the time they allotted themselves to do the job. Within five minutes, they were gone. They vanished as quickly as they arrived. The police weren't able to get there in time to stop them. The gang made off with over 400 of the best sweat suits money could buy. This was just another routine job for the gang, but what would happen after was anything but routine.

Ten days, later Jake called me and again asked me to stop by. This had become a routine by now, so I knew what was up. When I entered his basement, I expected more of the same, which was stolen merchandise. This time, the stolen sweat suits were on display. The only thing I wasn't expecting to see was the untrustworthy Ira Kilstein. And yet there he stood. I was fucking steaming mad. Chris Campanella told me to take what I wanted so I was extra quick when I picked out around ten sweat suits. I grabbed five for me and five for Vanessa. I didn't want Kilstein to know anything, so I told Jake I wanted to speak with him upstairs. He giggled and swore he wouldn't open his mouth. While we were in the Bahamas shooting the movie, I constantly preached to Jake of the dangers of being involved with Kilstein. It always fell on deaf ears. I was wasting my time beating that dead horse. After Maurice had robbed Jake's house, he threw all caution to the wind. He should really have circled the wagons and tightened up his inner circle.

In the meantime, I got out of Jake's as quick as I could and prayed Kilstein would forget I was there. Jake's next move would be a bad one and would start the dominoes falling down. He let Kilstein talk Chris Campanella into fronting him a hundred of the sweat suits on credit so he could sell them. Chris did, and it was the kiss of death. It would trigger a chain reaction of events that were all bad. Kilstein left with the sweat suits and began hustling them. He also started telling everyone where they came from. That was his problem; he never knew when to shut the fuck up! Anyhow, one thing led to another and Kilstein ended up fucking Chris out of this money. That was a bad move. You don't steal from these guys and get away with it. You just knew Chris was not going to let Kilstein get away with screwing him. Like I said, Jake made a horrible decision getting involved with Kilstein, and now it would cost him dearly. This is where all the soon to be problems started.

Chris Campanella was a devious bastard, and not long after Kilstein burned him, he plotted his revenge. Not only did the Crash and Carry Gang rob stores, they also robbed drug dealers. It wasn't even a week later that I received a call from Jake who told me he needed me to meet him at the racquetball club at 4:30 that same day. He stressed that it was really important. I knew something was up. When I got there, Chris Campanella was waiting there with him. They both looked like the cat that ate the mouse. They made sure we all signed in and that the employees noticed us. We were going to play some racquetball. When we got into the enclosed court, they told me why. They said we all needed alibis. I chuckled and realized something big was going down. While playing, Chris gave me a hint as to what was happening.

At 5:15, while Jake, Chris, and I were working up a sweat, two big guys who were friends of Chris' from the city were busy robbing Kilstein's house. The two guys posed as detectives and knocked on Kilstein's door. Kilstein's mother and wife were home so when they answered the door, the phony cops handcuffed them and waited for Ira to come home. Ira Kilstein was out with his father at the time. About 45 minutes later, Kilstein and his dad walked into a nightmare. They were quickly subdued by the robbers and were also handcuffed to a pole along with his wife and mother. The crooks forced Kilstein at gunpoint to open his safe. Inside was a kilo of cocaine and around fifty grand. There was also a shitload of jewelry. They took it all. Before they left, the phony cops began groping Kilstein's wife, squeezing her ass and titties. When they finished, they left.

With Kilstein and his family all handcuffed to a pole, they were trapped. If it hadn't been for one of Kilstein's customers stopping by, they might have been there for days. As this guy Roger knocked on Kilstein's door, he could hear the family screaming frantically for help. Roger let himself in and called the police. The cops were stunned when they arrived on the scene. They found Kilstein, his wife, his mother, and father all handcuffed to an iron pole in the basement. This was not your typical crime you normally saw in that upscale type of neighborhood. The detectives were furious. Things suddenly got deadly serious for everyone. A home invasion in broad daylight, holy shit. What is next?

When I got home around 7 o'clock that night, news was starting to come in. A friend of mine called me and told me that something big happened at Kilstein's. He said that there were news vans at Kilstein's house. I already knew what happened. It turned into a real circus. I don't think anyone anticipated the type of exposure it was about to get. It ended up airing on some of the major news stations. The next morning, it was in the papers. Kilstein was embarrassed and angry as hell so he wasted no time in throwing everyone under the bus.

Although Jake and I weren't responsible directly for what happened at Kilstein's, Ira automatically assumed we were involved so he really tried to stick it to us. The day after the robbery, detectives and the FBI went to Kilstein's to try and figure out who was behind it. For years, the FBI tried building a case against the Crash and Carry Gang without much success. As usual, they would come up short. Ira Kilstein was unable to identify anyone in the dozens of photos the cops and Feds showed him. They had no proof of anything, but did have a good idea about what took place and who was involved. Thanks to Kilstein's big mouth, the pieces would start to come together. That was the day a major investigation of all of us began. Ira ratted out every single one of us. He told the FBI and cops everything he knew about Jake, the robbery crew, and me. The cops, and especially the FBI, had enough of this shit. What they pieced together was a massive crime ring.

A friend of mine dropped by my house less than a week later, and he was frightened. He explained to me that he had just come from Kilstein's, and that he was there while the FBI was questioning Ira. The Feds had shown Ira some recent photos of me and some of my associates leaving Jake's house the past few days. The photos were actually taken the day before. We were all under round the clock surveillance. Hearing that, I decided to halt any further criminal activities for a while. I wanted to see if things would die down. Of course, they did not. I got followed everywhere.

After hearing that Kilstein was going to try to hang all of us, I grabbed a rental car and paid Jake a visit. He wasn't home, so I had to wait until the following day at our karate lesson to talk to him. When the lesson was over, I briefed him on the situation. I told him I was shutting it down for the time being, and that he should do the same. He half-heartedly said he would, but deep down I knew he couldn't. When you are caught up in the hustle game making easy money, it's almost impossible to voluntarily stop. It's just as hard to stop dealing drugs, as it is to stop using drugs. Making that money becomes just as addictive.

About two weeks later, I received a call and was asked if I wanted to join a bunch of the guys from our crew who were going to the city to party one night. Lucky for me, I declined. Now there is a reason I am not mentioning any names. The boys loaded up into the car and began the hour ride into Manhattan. They were going to visit our bouncer friend Sean McGuire at the club where he worked. After my really close call when I was almost stabbed by that hooker, none of us went into the city without packing a weapon. On this night, two of the four were carrying guns. We all could handle ourselves extremely well, but New York was a dangerous place so having some insurance was smart.

The night was fairly uneventful. The guys drank a lot, ate, and even danced with some women. Nothing happened really until it was time to leave. While in the club earlier, the guys exchanged hard stares with another crew of about five or six Guidos. No one did anything, so they thought it was over. When my boys went to leave and stepped outside, they saw the crew of Guidos in front of the club waiting for them. It was now around 3 A.M. Everyone was bombed so you could see where this was heading. Both groups once again started bickering back and forth. In seconds, it was on.

A ferocious fight broke out right on the sidewalk and in the street. My buddies made quick work of the other crew, whipping their ass easily. After a few minutes, the Guidos started running away and seemed to have had enough. My boys then walked to the front of the club and started talking to our friend Sean McGuire. The last thing my buddies expected was for the other group they had just fought to come back for more.

Minutes later, one of my boys turned around and saw those five guys double timing it back down the street to the club. Only this time the guys all had bats, sticks, and pipes. Finally, one of the guys from our crew said, "Fuck this." He pulled out his handgun and when they got close enough he opened fire. The gunfire shattered the late night calm. He fired multiple shots and dropped the two closest targets who were aggressively approaching him. The rest of the Guidos reversed course and hauled ass out of there. One of those fuckers was shot in the leg while the other less fortunate Guido was shot twice, once in the stomach and once in the balls. The guy who was shot twice stumbled across the street and fell behind a dumpster. My buddies then ran for the car around the corner, hopped in, and blazed home to Long Island. Before they left, they stopped on the 59th Street Bridge and threw the guns in the East River.

Back at the club, the police showed up just moments after the shooting. The guy who was shot in the leg fell right in the street where he was shot, so paramedics began attending to him first. They didn't even see the guy who had been shot in the balls and stomach. He was in grave condition. About three minutes later, one of the officers noticed a pair of feet sticking out from underneath the dumpster. It was very reminiscent of the scene in the Wizard of

Oz where the witch had the house fall on her and all you could see were her legs. Both men were taken away in ambulances. The guy who was injured worse turned out to be the son of some former big time city official. The police questioned the bouncers and some witnesses. None of the bouncers said a word about anything because they knew we were good friends with one of their coworkers. Some of the witnesses claimed the Westies did it due to the fact that my buddies who were involved were mostly Irish. The boys made it back safely to Long Island without getting picked up by the police.

I heard about the melee the next afternoon. I didn't realize how crazy everything that happened was until someone who was there described it to me in detail. My father added to the festivities when he came in from work and dropped a newspaper down. My dad pointed out an article that highlighted the ordeal. My father kept it because he recognized the name of the club where everything happened. His jaw dropped when I informed him that my buddies were involved. It didn't shock my dad at all when he found out.

Things quieted down shortly afterward, and I really tried to make myself invisible for a while. Jake, instead of following my lead, went right back to slinging cocaine. Even after Kilstein getting robbed, which brought the heat of the FBI around, he wasn't deterred by all of the law enforcement presence. It wasn't a smart idea. I kept pleading with him to shut it down but he wouldn't listen. Jake even brought a few new players into the fold.

One of the new players was a massive man we called, "Big Ray Scalzo." He was a major criminal who was known for his specialty, which was robbing or rolling drug dealers. I will tell you more about Big Ray, just not yet. Instead of everything settling down, things got crazier and crazier. Jake was now totally out of control and making bad decisions one after another. While he operated in the spotlight, I pulled back the reigns and started collecting a lot of the money I had on the street. I could see a major storm was heading everyone's way, and I wanted to have as few loose ends as possible. And I did it at exactly the right time.

In this business you have to be extremely vigilant, and I always could see the big picture. I tried to avoid going over to Jake's for the time being and only really saw him at our daily karate lessons that he was starting to lose interest in. Jake was changing and definitely for the worse. We had trained together for a long time and had been in the drug business together since 1985. But in this business you had to be able to read the signs if you wanted to stay in business. The signs I was reading were all bad. Jake was oblivious to everything though, either that or he just didn't give a fuck. You needed major balls to be in this line of work, but having balls meant nothing if you weren't smart. And I was very smart. I remember seeing one of my pals right after he came back from Jake's. He described a house full of over a dozen hardcore criminals, all packing pieces and talking about robbing people. They were even shooting off guns right in Jake's backyard. I told him, "This was the beginning of the end." If you actually stepped back and analyzed the overall situation, it was pretty easy to see what was going to happen.

It wouldn't be long now before the curtain would fall on this three-ring circus that had been rolling along for almost seven years. Kilstein's house had been robbed maybe three or four months earlier. Most of the crew had by now forgotten about that, and the fact that Kilstein had boasted to anyone who would listen that we were all going to jail. I, on the other hand, never forgot. For a while now, I really pulled back and tried to shield myself from the inexorable fallout that was certainly coming. It was a lot harder to stop hustling than one may realize. I had gotten so used to the everyday grind where I was making such easy money. But I had more than enough cash put aside, so I realized it wasn't worth the risk of losing everything. Jake couldn't stop anymore. He had tunnel vision, and just never processed how serious things had become. Couple that with the fact that his house was now a haven for all kinds of wanted criminals. You could almost write the ending now. But I will do the honors and tell you how it all shook out.

Winter was now slamming the New York area hard. December 1990 was cold and gray, but it did not curb the nonstop activity going on at Jake's. There was a constant stream of traffic coming and going all day and night. He would have all types of people around like Big Ray who were either plotting robberies or buying drugs. A lot of the business was conducted while playing pool in the upstairs bedroom. Man, if those walls could talk. I was doing a lot of keeping to myself and had been for months now.

My business was completely shut down, and I was enjoying my time off. I even relocated to a new apartment close to the old ski lodge called High Point. Vanessa and I reconnected during my stand down, and she was happy to have my undivided attention for the first time in a long time. Jake's business was booming big time, but he wasn't paying close enough attention to his surroundings. He was completely unaware that while his house was buzzing with activity, he was under surveillance full time. The local police precinct had undercovers sitting on his crib constantly. Jake never talked on the phone, so they weren't going to get him like that. The cops would have to pull someone over leaving his house and catch them with something. If they could nail someone pulling away, they would then try to pressure them into becoming an informant. Once someone flips, the cops usually make them go back and do a buy for them. And once that happens, the police can get a search warrant. Although people were scared to death of us, you never knew how someone was going to react when they are caught with narcotics and facing jail time.

The calendar year had again turned, and we were now into January 1991. The month went by slowly, and nothing seemed to be wrong or out of the ordinary. However, unbeknownst to Jake, one of his customers, a guy by the name of William Jackson whom he had known since high school had gotten pulled over leaving Jake's house one night, about five days before the Giants were to play the Bills in the Super Bowl. The cops got lucky and nailed the right guy. The other fifty customers of Jake's would never have talked, but this guy did. William was caught with an eight ball of cocaine and some pills. The cops scared the shit out of him telling him he was going to jail for years, and that was all it took to get him to roll over. Had he kept his mouth shut, Jake would have paid for a lawyer for him, and he wouldn't have done a day in jail because he had no record. He had never been arrested, so he panicked. Now the police had what they needed to take Jake down.

That Friday, Jake decided to take a trip to Atlantic City to gamble and watch the Super Bowl. It was the first time in history that two New York teams would play each other in the big game. While Jake was going to be in Atlantic City, he was stupid enough to leave his girlfriend Tina in charge of taking care of customers while he was away. It was a horrendous move. I never understood that decision, but he did it and that's that.

On Saturday, while Jake was in the middle of losing money at the blackjack tables, the police were busy planting a wire on William Jackson and getting ready to send him into Jake's house to make a buy for them. They were also in the process of obtaining a search warrant for the house. An hour later, while the police were sitting a few houses down, William Jackson knocked nervously on Jake's door and waited for Jake to answer. To his surprise, Jake's woman greeted him when the door opened. Like a weasel, he smiled and stepped inside. He followed Tina to the basement and down the stairs. She pulled out a huge bag of cocaine, and cut him up an eight ball on the digital scale. Tina had no clue she was selling to a police informant. After she gave it to him, Jackson handed over $200 in marked bills. That was it, her ticket to jail was just punched. William Jackson had just totally backstabbed people he knew for years, people who have looked out for him. It was irrelevant because he only cared about his own troubles. I wonder if he ever thought about how much trouble he was about to bring to someone who considered him a friend. I guess in the end, it really didn't matter.

When most of us awoke on Sunday, January 27, 1991, none of us expected the wild day that was in store. The majority of people in the New York area were busy making plans to watch Super Bowl XXV. I did a really good workout and then ran a few miles that afternoon before settling in for the big game. It was now getting close to kickoff time. As most of America was concentrating on the game and getting their bets in, the Fourth Precinct Police Department along with a Narcotics Task Force was getting ready to raid Jake's house not long after kickoff. The funny thing was, no one was home. The police did not know that, though. They probably assumed there would be some huge get together there when they arrived.

Not long after the game started, in what would be a tremendous Super Bowl, the police began organizing everything they needed to do tactically. They were only a block away. It was now 7 P.M. Less than ten minutes later, over a dozen vehicles pulled up right in front of Jake's house and a good 25-30 officers quickly jumped out, and without knocking, blew Jake's door down with a battering ram. They entered the empty house with their guns drawn. Then the dogs came in. Earlier that day, Jake's girlfriend Tina left to go out and locked up the cocaine in a safe in Jake's bedroom. The dogs sniffed it out immediately. When the cops opened the safe, they discovered almost a kilo of cocaine, $67,000 in cash and thousands of pharmaceuticals. They also found two unregistered handguns. While the police ripped Jake's house apart, he was in Atlantic City having a great time and had no idea his world was about to come crashing down hard.

About an hour later, Tina came back to the house. She almost fainted when she pulled close to the house and saw cops everywhere. Horrified, she never even slowed down and passed right by, unsure of what to do. Our good buddy Brian Bartholameau was at the house right behind Jake's watching the Super Bowl. Tina saw Brian's truck and pulled in to tell him what happened.

Brian let her in, they beeped Jake in Atlantic City, and waited anxiously for his call back. Two or three minutes later, Jake called and they broke the bad news to him. He was devastated. One thing became crystal clear, from that point forward nothing would be the same for any of us again!

Part II

If You Can't Beat 'Em, Join 'Em

As I sat watching the last second field goal attempt by the Buffalo Bills kicker Scott Norwood sail wide right, which would ultimately catapult the New York Giants to Super Bowl XXV champions, a good friend of mine named Brian Bartholameau was racing over to my apartment in Huntington to pass along the bad news about what happed at Jake's. Maybe fifteen minutes after the game ended, he knocked on my door. With him was Jake's girlfriend Tina. They were both distraught. I let them in, we sat down in my living room, and they began to fill me in.

I can't say it surprised me in the least, because everything I had seen pointed to this outcome. What we didn't know yet, but assumed, was there were now felony arrest warrants out for Jake and Tina. They were for felony sale of a controlled substance, possession with intent to distribute, conspiracy, and possession of two handguns. There were also a shitload of lesser charges. When Jake heard the catastrophic news while in Atlantic City, he decided to take off to Georgia. His parents had a condo there that was unoccupied most of the year. The plan for him was to have his girl meet him down there, and then try to figure out his next move.

The first thing that popped into my mind while listening to Brian and Tina recount the ordeal, was, *Who's next?* I assumed the worst, and was wondering if they would roll up our entire crew at once. But I kept my composure and really thought it through. There was quite an interesting twist to this story, though. Brian began to tell me in detail the insanity of what he did. Brian was a good ten years older than all of us. He had a brother who was doing twenty to life for killing someone during a robbery that went bad, so his family was no stranger to the criminal justice system.

Brian had just beat an assault rap in Suffolk County that he was on trial for. When he sat down with his lawyer on day one of the trial, he looked over at the twelve jurors and was stunned. Sitting there amongst the jurors was a friend of ours we called Fitzy. Fitzy was a schoolteacher who was out of his mind. Earlier in life, Jake had dosed Fitzy with a vial of liquid LSD, and it completely blew his mind. Fitzy went on about a six-month trip from the acid and almost never came out of it. After seeing Fitzy on the jury, Brian knew he had nothing to worry about. When the trial was over, Brian was acquitted in an hour.

Now Brian told me what went on at Jake's. When Brian talked to Jake in Atlantic City, Jake told him that there was another half kilo of coke he had stashed under the deck in the backyard. There were two Rottweilers in Jake's backyard at the time. For whatever reason, the cops never went into the backyard at all when they raided the house. No one in their right mind would try to go back there to retrieve the coke, right? Wrong. That fucking maniac Brian did just that. While the house was swarming with cops everywhere, that sick bastard, with the stealth of a ninja, hopped the back fence and then low crawled on his belly a good twenty yards, and snuck under the deck. He found the coke that was left there. It was buried in coffee cans. When he was under the deck, he along with the dogs who were by now licking his face, observed the police through the small basement window for about ten minutes. Brian realized he shouldn't push his luck and quietly exited the premises. He then grabbed Tina and headed for my house. I was amazed at the balls it took to do what he did. Brian and I laughed our asses off over that, in what was no amusing situation.

When Brian and Jake's woman left, it really started to sink in just how potentially serious everything could be. Unfortunately, I would have to sit back to see how this would unfold. Word spread swiftly of Jake's house getting raided, so loyal customers of his started to flock over to Ira Kilstein's before Jake's body was even cold. That's the harsh reality of life in the hustle game. A couple of days later, I got word of something that pissed me the fuck off. I heard that the day after the raid at Jake's, Kilstein and Rich Reikert were at the Clubhouse, toasting with champagne, the fact that Jake was now eliminated from the equation.

And Kilstein was the scumbag who caused it all. He was also banking on the fact that me and the rest of our crew would be taken down as well. His wish was never granted. The next few weeks were really stressful not knowing if there was going to be a knock at my door by the cops or Feds. It weighed heavily on my mind. The big thing was that the police had let Jake and his girl slip right through their fingers and ended up arresting nobody. It is almost hard to believe it happened, but there is always some incompetence when it comes to law enforcement. That only made the cops that more intent on not making that mistake again. I did not want to be their consolation prize. The games were only just beginning.

Some time passed, and I would use my time moving forward to try to analyze everything as best I could, so I could eventually regroup. It had been months now since I did any hustling. I started to get the feeling that if the cops were going to arrest me, it would have happened already. Detectives had been to Jake's parents' house many times by now, trying to harass them into turning their son in. Jake's parents were big time Christians and didn't like crime. But he was still their son, so even if they did know where Jake was, they would never tell. In the beginning, Jake kept everyone in the dark of his whereabouts, except me. Tina was now with Jake, and they were still at the condo so they knew they had to move far away and hopefully avoid the long arm of the law. They were a real life Bonnie & Clyde. After months of laying low, the couple decided to move out west to California. It was a wise move on their part. Jake was now officially "on the lamb," a wanted criminal with multiple felony arrest warrants out for him. He would have to be extremely careful with anything he did from here on in, even something as small as speeding or blowing a stop sign could be the end of him. His life was going to change drastically. And he was looking at a potential twenty-year sentence back in New York.

Some time after the bust at Jake's, his brother Carl and the guy I mentioned earlier, Big Ray, stopped by my apartment. I had been friends with Carl for many years, but only knew Big Ray a short time. Big Ray was a hardened criminal who was brought up from his college in Maryland by some of the Crash and Carry Gang. He was an intimidating and physically imposing man. Standing 6 foot 4 inches, and weighing 375, he looked like a grizzly bear. Big Ray played Division I college football. He played defensive tackle. His specialty was armed robbery. Dozens and dozens of drug dealers in Maryland and up and down the East Coast, would have the unfortunate luck of being robbed by him.

I was apprehensive initially meeting him and becoming involved with him, but he started to grow on me. Big Ray could easily have been cast in the show "The Sopranos" because he was a total character. He was Italian and not only could he also talk the talk, he walked the walk as a real gangster. We didn't know it yet, but Big Ray and I would eventually become inseparable and involved in something so devious it would be right on par with what notorious gangster Whitey Bulger pulled off years earlier. The difference being that Bulger was in his 50s or 60s when he did it, and we were only in our early to mid 20s.

First things first, we let a few months pass and we called Jake out in California. He had thousands of dollars on the street that needed to be collected, and by now those customers assumed they weren't going to have to pay up because Jake was gone. Boy, were they wrong. I was an extremely loyal friend of Jake's and knew he needed some help with getting his dough. He was now surviving on pocket change. I told Jake, "I got you, bro." I grabbed Big Ray and Big Charles, who was another 6 foot 5 inch, 275 pound monster. The three of us started paying visits to people who were on the list Jake gave me. I remember the look on J.P.'s face when he opened the door to the terrifying site of the three of us staring him down. He turned white as a sheet and couldn't speak.

J.P. owed Jake three grand. I read him the riot act and gave him until Friday to pay up, or I told him we would be back. It was now Monday. Not even 24 hours later J.P. was at Jake's father's house dropping off every cent he owed. Almost everyone we visited followed suit. They couldn't get caught up quickly enough. There were some people we had trouble tracking down, but after word of the goon squad, making visits to collect some of them got so spooked, we never saw them again.

Our buddy Brian Bartholameau was initially ordered by Jake to give the half kilo of coke that he got from under Jake's house to Big Ray, so he could start blowing it out to some of Jake's old customers. Big Ray and Jake's brother Carl had moved back into Jake's old house in Commack, and had the audacity to start hustling again from the same place that was busted only a short time ago. This was really risky. And the customers began returning. The police must have been in shock when news of the activity at the house got back to them. It took some nerve by Big Ray to even think about it, much less, do it. But Big Ray said, "Fuck it." And did it anyway.

Almost immediately, people started getting pulled over leaving the house, so if Big Ray wanted to stay in business, he had to move. Just before he did move, something bizarre happened at the house. One night around 8 P.M., Big Ray was watching TV in the living room. Jake's brother was in the apartment of the house literally with his pants down, rubbing one out. The front door came flying open, and there were three guys with guns claiming to be police. They ordered Big Ray to get on the floor, and he did. While one of the crooks stood over Big Ray, the other two kicked in the apartment door where Jake's brother was busy jerking off. The phony cops must have been surprised at the sight of Carl with his dick in his hand. They walked Carl to the living room, and threatened for them to hand over the money and drugs. Both Big Ray and Carl were in disbelief. They began laughing and told the robbers that the house had been raided only months earlier. The crooks didn't believe them and started ripping the house apart. They found nothing. Only a few feet away there was the 8 ounces of coke under the couch cushion, but they never looked there. The robbers left after an hour, and Big Ray called the police. When detectives showed up, they couldn't believe this type of shit was still going on. They were anything but helpful. Big Ray said enough is enough and packed up shop and moved to Syosset to a safer location.

Back at my place, I was dealing with my own problems. My girlfriend Vanessa was again becoming totally out of control with the pills. This was the last thing I needed because there was still some heat around. From time to time, I was still being followed. This was not the type of headache I needed right about now. But things would continue to get worse. Vanessa could have cared less about putting me in potential danger; the only thing that mattered was her getting her fix. And I was stupid enough to enable her. It is tough, when you love someone, you sometimes make decisions with your heart and not with your head. And that was exactly what I did. She pestered me daily, sometimes hourly for the damn things. I always had a good supply of pharmaceuticals around, and she knew it. On occasion, I would take them myself, but I tried my hardest to stay disciplined with them, knowing the dangers of physical addiction. With Vanessa, it became a losing battle I was waging. Trying to control someone else's drug usage is a complete waste of time when you are dealing with an addict.

Vanessa's drug problem was dormant for a little while, but now it was rearing its ugly head again. And this was just the beginning. Shortly after she became enamored with the painkillers, she started with the cocaine again also. It was a double whammy. She just put the peddle to the floor. Like an idiot, I started buying her an eight ball a day. Couple that with the fifty or so Percocet she was taking each day, and she was off to the races. She became a runaway locomotive that was going to destroy everything in its path. I had my hands full. Her good time was costing me $2,000 a week. I made her pay me back in non-monetary ways. For all the aggravation she was giving me, I would take out my frustrations in all kinds of kinky ways in the bedroom.

During my stand down from hustling, I used that time to strategize my comeback. I had somewhat of a cerebral approach to the drug business and always tried to look at every angle while operating. It's probably the reason I didn't get caught up with Jake's troubles when he went down. Something happened in early April that gave me an idea that was brilliant. Jake's brother Carl was over a former customer of mine's house named Craig when a plain clothed police officer they knew stopped by. The cop's name was Curt Vandenberg.

This cop hated Ira Kilstein with a passion and wanted his ass gone. Officer Vandenberg knew Kilstein used ratting out Jake as a power play to take control of the cocaine business around Huntington. Vandenberg wanted Carl's help in taking down Kilstein. Carl explained to Officer Vandenberg that he would love to help, but that he really needed to talk to me to be able to pull it off. After he thought about it for a minute, he said, "Okay, talk to Patrick and see what he says." Carl said he would. Thus, the die was cast. That chance encounter between the two of them would lead to an epic alliance of the most unlikely parties.

Carl woke up the next day, called me, said he needed me to come over to his parents' house, and that it was urgent. I was curious as to why. When I pulled up to his parents' house, Carl was standing there with a glass of orange juice in one hand while calmly smoking a cigarette with the other. He took his last drag of it and stepped on it to put it out, while flashing an evil grin my way. Without having said anything, I knew this was going to be good. Jake's brother Carl then told me in detail of this run in with Officer Vandenberg, and his plan to pay Kilstein back for getting Jake busted. It definitely got my attention, so we continued our conversation. Carl made it very clear that the cops would need my help in making it happen. The reason being was that I knew Ira Kilstein's operation in and out. I knew who almost all of his customers were, including having a lot of their beeper numbers and phone numbers. My knowledge of everything is what was needed to get the police all of the pertinent information to put this whole thing together. I told Carl I would think about it and said, "I'll let you know tomorrow." Driving home, my mind started envisioning the whole scenario. Getting involved with the police was the last thing I ever imagined doing at that time.

Something then struck me all of a sudden. This could be a great thing, and the timing couldn't have been better. As I said much earlier, to be in this business you not only had to be smart but ruthless. Only one thing counts, and that is survival. The currents have shifted with the whole dealing scene overnight in Huntington. And I was about to make a calculated and sinister move to ensure my safety that would enable me to start dealing again and well into the future.

Pulling in my driveway, I noticed a little red Toyota car sitting in front of my place. Then I saw a familiar face sitting on my steps. It was one of my weed connects, Fast Frankie. We hadn't seen each other in months. Fast Frankie had heard about Jake having gotten busted, and he wanted to make sure I was okay. After shaking hands, I gave him the scoop on everything. He had taken some time off also but was ready to start doing things again. My ears were wide open, and I listened to his pitch. I said, "Fuckin' A," and responded, "let's do this."

I was through with the cocaine business. It brought so much bad karma, and the police were targeting coke dealers more than anyone else. Fast Frankie and I finished making arrangements for the following week and then we said goodbye. I stepped into my house and smiled. I was about to go over to the dark side and become a police informant. Now I had no love for the cops, but I was smart enough to know if I didn't take some precautionary steps, my hustling career would be a short one.

My plan was to meet with the cops who would be involved in this operation they had planned, get in good with them, and then start systematically dispatching of all of our competition by ratting out anyone who stood in our way. A lot of things would have to happen in order to do this right. I would have to talk this over with my new partner in crime, Big Ray, before giving Carl the green light to tell Officer Vandenberg we were on board. Big Ray loved my idea and wanted in. After all, he was selling cocaine, so buying himself some insurance would be a wise move.

That Thursday I would finally meet the man who would piece everything together on the law enforcement side. And that was Officer Curt Vandenberg. As I walked into Carl's parents' house, I stepped up into the living room and saw Carl and Officer Vandenberg sitting on a white leather couch. Curt got up, and we looked each other dead in the eye. Officer Vandenberg was a strikingly handsome man and looked a lot like the actor Gabriel Byrne. His eyes were blue and he had wavy brown hair. I was greeted by a firm handshake from him. While shaking my hand, he smiled and said, "Patrick I've been trying to bust you for years."

"You must not have been too successful, " I replied. We both broke into laughter. It was a great way to break the ice. There was something I liked right away about the guy. Officer Vandenberg went on to tell me how many people were caught leaving my house with drugs on them, but they always refused to cooperate. As long as he was a cop, he said he had never seen people so afraid of anyone as they were of me.

The cop also explained to me that my neighbors called on me almost daily, complaining about the traffic at my house. "The police were very frustrated with your situation," Curt told me. I informed him that I quit the coke business, but that I still sold weed. Officer Vandenberg said, "I didn't care about weed, and I could live with that." He knew he was making a deal with the devil, so he expected there would be some strings attached. For my cooperation, he had to look the other way with some of my indiscretions. The weed dealing was one of them. "No problem," he said. I also let him know that Big Ray wanted in on the action with me. Vandenberg said, "I'll talk to him." The last thing Curt said to me, "If you are straight with me, I'll be straight with you." I never forgot that. And he ended up being a real straight shooter. This was the beginning of a beautiful friendship.

When I pulled away from Carl's in my Cadillac, I exhaled and said, "Wow." In my hand was Curt's card with his beeper number and phone number on it. He told me to call him anytime. I had to pinch myself because I couldn't believe this was really happening. It was, and there was no backing out now. Risky was a word you could use to describe my plan. For all I knew, the cops could have been playing me and the whole thing could end up backfiring. Well, I guess we will just have to see.

The next day, when Big Ray left his apartment in Syosset, he was going to be surprised. I had been unable to reach him after my meeting the previous day with Officer Vandenberg. Big Ray lived in a wooded area, so when he pulled out of his driveway to head to Huntington to make a delivery, he didn't notice the undercover vehicle sitting a few houses down. The thick bushes on the side of the road hid it. As Big Ray started down the narrow street, he looked in his rear view mirror and saw he was being followed. In seconds, lights started flashing from the plain white sedan behind him. An arm was signaling from the undercover vehicle for him to pull over. "What the fuck is this?" Big Ray yelled to himself as he stopped the car. He had a pound of marijuana on the front seat. As he looked back, he saw Officer Vandenberg getting out of the undercover car.

They had already made each other's acquaintances once before when Curt Vandenberg pulled him over after leaving one of his customer's houses in Huntington. It was a real close call. Big Ray had just dropped off an ounce of coke to a client, so all Officer Vandenberg found on him was some cash. Not knowing I had already arranged everything, Big Ray assumed he was busted with the weed this time. When Officer Vandenberg got close to Big Ray's car, Big Ray jumped out and threw the pound of weed on the roof of the car and said, "You got me." Shockingly, Officer Vandenberg told Big Ray, "Put that shit away, you fucking idiot." Big Ray then threw the marijuana under the seat. Curt then let Big Ray know he just wanted to talk to him and fill him in on the situation with Kilstein and about our plan. Ray was giddy. After talking for thirty minutes, they parted ways, and Officer Vandenberg said he would be in touch. Big Ray suddenly realized the same thing I did, and that was this could work out great if we played our cards right.

My customers were all starving by now. I broke the bad news to them, telling them that I would no longer be selling cocaine anymore. That business went to Big Ray from now on. The people who sold weed were happy to find out that I was back in business with the pot again. Fast Frankie had just dropped off 100 pounds of some really good smoke to my apartment. I broke it up on a new scale that I had just bought for $700. Most of the pot was wrapped up and shipped to my buddies in college. The rest I pieced out and sold locally. Things picked up so fast it almost felt as if I never stopped. Everyone was again happy. What I would do was pick up a load, flip it quickly, and then take a little time off to see if everything was okay. My ear was to the ground constantly trying to pick up on what was going on around town. After a while, I figured out that as long as I worked for the police, I was untouchable. My new comrades on the force were not going to let anything happen to me with such a huge investigation taking place. They had their priorities in order.

Within four or five days, Officer Vandenberg called me at home and said he was setting up a meeting with the Drug Enforcement Agency. He wanted to know if I was okay with it. I said, "Hell yeah, Curt. You just let me know where and when," I replied. He also called Big Ray. My phone rang back an hour later, and Officer Vandenberg told me we were all going to be at some fancy restaurant in Syosset. The DEA was going to spring for dinner while we all got acquainted with one another.

Big Ray and I showed up at 7:30 P.M. to the restaurant. Officer Vandenberg and the DEA agents were already there. Curt introduced all of us. The two agents were named Joe and Bob. I gave them nicknames right away. Joe who I would call "Joe Weider" was a stocky 5 foot 11 inch, 250 pound Italian who was built like a brick shit-house. He sported two or three gold chains in true Guido fashion. The other guy Bob I nicknamed "Bob Hawaii," because he wore one of those flowered Hawaiian shirts while wearing sunglasses at night. They were straight out of Hollywood's central casting. You could tell they were narcs a mile away. The agents were all business, though. These were the types of guys who would wake up and salute the flag before they even left for work. Drugs were something they despised, and the only thing they hated more than drugs were drug dealers.

At first, they were kind of reluctant to get involved, but after meeting with us they loosened up a bit. They had no sense of humor and were stiff as a board. We enjoyed a great meal on their dime and talked for two hours. Ira Kilstein was the major topic of conversation. Agents Joe and Bob wanted to know everything. I brought with me a list of everyone involved with Kilstein, including addresses, beeper numbers, and phone numbers. Officer Vandenberg explained to me later on that the reason he brought the DEA on board was that they had much better seizure abilities. They were going to clean house when all was said and done. The DEA hated to admit it, but they needed Big Ray and me to bring this to a head.

Once the meal was done, the agents gave Big Ray and me their cards. In my wallet, I now had both agents' cards and Officer Vandenberg's card. They were essentially "get out of jail free" cards. Big Ray and I left, grabbed coffee on the way home, and discussed our evening. While sipping our coffee, we decided we would use this force field around us to build our businesses up. We were going to totally exploit the situation to our benefit. Everything was now official; we were full time rats. It may sound cold but in this world, it's kill, or be killed. All we did was take a preemptive strike against our enemies. Hell, Kilstein already ratted my crew and me out. We were just returning the favor, the only difference being we would do it right.

Shortly after the investigation kicked off, our loyalty to each other would be tested. I mean between Big Ray, the cops, and me. One day, while Big Ray and I were driving through the Pathmark shopping center in Dix Hills, we spotted someone who owed a lot of money. Big Ray slammed on the brakes, and we both jumped out and cornered this punk. His eyes were bulging with fear. We slammed him up against the window of a hair salon and started working him over. The Second Precinct was only four blocks away. Someone in the hair salon called 911, and within two minutes there were four cop cars on the scene. Seeing this guy was beat up, the cops slapped handcuffs on Big Ray and me.

I pulled one of the officers aside and told him to go into my wallet and take out Officer Vandenberg's card. He was surprised to learn that I knew him. Lucky for us, Vandenberg was working that day. The uniformed cop radioed Curt and he told them to release us immediately. To the officer's dismay, he had no choice but to listen to Curt. They uncuffed Big Ray and me and actually apologized for the mix up. It then sank in just how important we had become. This was sweet. We called Jake in California, and told him about our diabolical scheme to pay Kilstein back. Jake said, "You guys are insane, but I love it." Jake's life was ruined. He was now working some minimum wage job and was barely getting by. We told Jake we would get back to him soon.

Exactly seven days after meeting with the DEA, Officer Vandenberg stopped by my crib letting me know that the following evening the DEA agents needed Big Ray and me to do something with them. I said, "Sure." When the next night arrived, Big Ray and I were waiting on my steps when a white van with blackened out windows pulled up and stopped in front of my apartment. The side door opened and there was Officer Vandenberg sitting in one of the back seats. He yelled, "Get in," and we did. The two DEA agents were in the front seats.

"How you doing?" asked Agent Joe Weider. "Good," we replied. Officer Vandenberg then told us we were about to do some surveillance with them. Wow, amazing. We were actually about to drive around in a DEA spy van with the Feds and eyeball some criminals. It was surreal. Our first stop was going to be down the block from Kilstein's. We parked maybe two houses down from his. The agents then jumped in the back with us and put up this fake wall so no one could see in the back. We observed as people began coming and going, nonstop while running into Kilstein's buying cocaine. Joe Weider was watching with these really powerful binoculars. He would occasionally hand them to me to have a look. As each person left, Agent Weider asked me to identify them, and give him the scoop as to their business. I gave him as much as I could. Big Ray couldn't believe what we were doing. This was the type of shit you saw in the movies, only for us this was very real. The agents snapped some pictures, and we left after an hour.

The next stop was at another big coke dealer's house who was involved with Kilstein, named Rich Reikert. We parked almost at the end of his long driveway. Just like at Kilstein's, people were coming and going. We again watched everything. Forty minutes later, we saw my old boss J.P. leaving Reikert's, and we followed him. J.P. sold cocaine out of a few local bars when he wasn't landscaping. He had not a clue that we were following him. This imbecile then pulled into the 7-11 parking lot on Jericho Turnpike and began cutting up lines of cocaine on his dashboard. We were parked right next to him and watched him start sniffing the coke. As if things couldn't get stranger, J.P. got out of his car, and before going into the store, he walks up to the van and starts combing his hair in the window. It was my window. I was literally six inches from him. Thanks to that special tint, he couldn't see in. It was crazy. When he left 7-11, we followed him into a bar called Backstreets. The two agents inconspicuously trailed him into the establishment. There only fifteen minutes, the agents witnessed J.P. making hand-to-hand transactions right in the open. It's amazing how dumb these people were. They were almost begging to get arrested. The agents had seen enough, and we called it a night.

Big Ray was a total practical joker. He loved breaking people's balls, including mine. He had a real easy-going nature, which was hard to believe considering what a ruthless gangster he was. Sitting in his apartment one night while watching a ball game, he turns to me with this evil smile on his face and says, "Let's start tormenting Agents Joe Weider and Bob Hawaii." I giggled and asked him what he had in mind. Being so uptight, they made themselves such easy targets.

So Big Ray tells me he has an idea. Since we had their beeper numbers, he wanted to fuck with them a little. Back in 1991, there were these phone numbers that were advertised on TV constantly. You could call the numbers, and some woman would answer the phone and talk dirty to you, which is basically phone sex. One of the numbers was 976-FUCK. On a strange night, while doing a kilo of heroin buy and bust up in the South Bronx, Agent Joe Weider got a hit on his pager. Big Ray had beeped the 976-FUCK number into Joe Weider's beeper with a 911 after it. Agent Weider stopped what he was doing, ran to a certain phone they used, and returned the call from the page he had gotten. He was surprised when on the other end of the line a woman said, "I want to suck your balls and dick, big boy." Agent Weider lost it and started cursing the lady out. Raging mad, he slammed down the phone and went back to his business. An hour later, Big Ray did it again with another number, only this time to Bob Hawaii. Agent Hawaii called back and had the same thing happen to him. I told Ray to cool it. Oddly the next day, I got a call from Officer Vandenberg who told me about Agent Weider's crank calls that almost fucked up his deals the night before. The DEA agents thought we were behind it, and they were right. "If we find out those fucks are behind it, we are going to hang them," said Agent Weider to Vandenberg.

"It wasn't us," I told Vandenberg.

He laughed and said, "Please don't do it again." So, of course, we did.

The Fourth of July was only days away. Jake called me about three days before it and told me about an idea that he had. I had informed him a while back of everything we had going on with the cops and Feds. Jake remembered that I told him that Kilstein was now hiding his money at his mother-in-law's house, so his idea was to rob Kilstein again before the Feds could get the money. Some of the Crash and Carry Gang would be the ones to do it. Jake asked me to get the address of Kilstein's mother-in law's house. That night, I called him back and gave it to him. I told Jake that Kilstein was having a huge party at his house on the Fourth. Hundreds of people would be there, including Kilstein's wife's parents. It was perfect. So Jake contacted the gang and set everything up. Me, I just helped them out for shits and giggles.

On the afternoon of Independence Day, it was scorching hot. The drinks were flowing, and the music was blasting at Kilstein's house as people were partying hard. Having been robbed once already, I am sure that was the last thing on Kilstein's mind as he continued to slam pina coladas one after the other. However, as the party raged on at one residence, three phantom figures were entering the house where Kilstein now kept his cash from his drug proceeds. Once inside, the robbers were astounded to find an old grandmother in the kitchen. No one was supposed to be home. The 75-year old woman must have been startled big time. The crooks told granny she would not be harmed, but they did lock her in the closet temporarily. They went straight for the basement and saw a good size safe. It took all three of them to carry it out of the house. Before leaving, they let granny out of the closet. Not long after the gang left, the police were called. Officer Vandenberg learned of the robbery later that day, and he was not happy. Kilstein was in utter disbelief when the cops told him he had been robbed again. The take from the robbery was about $80,000.

Beep beep beep beep. My pager started going off as I sat down to eat dinner a few days later. Dusk was settling in over New York on a beautiful evening. There was a nice breeze in the air. The number of my pager was a California area code so I knew it was Jake. Deciding to leave my car home, I started to walk the short distance to the Dix Hills Diner to return his call. Walking quickly down the hill on my block, I came to the end, made a right on the next block, and continued walking.

Suddenly, a charcoal grey Monte Carlo with tinted windows skidded up to me in the sand, narrowly almost clipping me. The door swung open, and it was Agents Joe Weider and Bob Hawaii in the front. Officer Vandenberg was in the back seat behind the driver side. Scowls were on all of their faces. Angrily, a voice shouted, "Get the fuck in." I said to myself, *Oh shit, this can't be good.* Slightly hesitating, I jumped in the back seat, and the door slammed behind me. The tension in the air was so thick you could have cut it with a knife. We drove past the diner on Dix Hills Road and continued about another mile and a half down the street.

Agent Joe Weider then slammed on the brakes, and the car came to a screeching halt. If looks could kill, I would have been dead right there. Spinning to his right, Agent Weider turned to me and started verbally threatening me and tearing me a new asshole. He said, "I think it's funny that you told us Kilstein kept his money at his mother-in-law's house, and out of nowhere, it got robbed." Spit was literally flying out of his mouth he was so angry and out of control. He was speaking so fast I could barely make out what he was saying during his tantrum.

I calmly looked at Officer Vandenberg, and said, "I don't know what the hell you guys are talking about."

"You fucking lying scumbag," Agent Weider screamed.

Vandenberg smirked and said, "Sure you don't."

Suburban Gangsters

After a good ten minutes of being yelled at and threatened, Agent Joe Weider said, "Now get the fuck out, asshole." I hopped out of the car, and they sped away. That cocksucker made me walk almost two miles to get back home. At least Officer Vandenberg called me that night to apologize for what happened. He was actually being pretty cool considering. They still needed me to help them with what would turn out to be a massive investigation, so he didn't want to jeopardize it over something that wasn't that important in the overall grand scheme of things. On the other hand, the DEA agents hated us after that. They knew they were dealing with major criminals and hated the fact that they needed us to help make their case. What I came away with was that we had them dangling like puppets on a string, and Big Ray and I were the puppeteers.

Checking in almost daily with Officer Vandenberg became my responsibility. He wanted to know every little piece of intel I could get. And I was a treasure trove of information. Vandenberg was very impressed with my investigative skills. He and I started to develop a strong bond over time, and I would soon find out he was a real stand-up guy. There aren't many people I can say that about, but he was definitely one of them. What I didn't realize was how big this investigation would become. The state police were now brought into the fold as local cops, the state police, and the Feds were now monitoring this. It was hard to believe what we started. Officer Vandenberg was a real ambitious guy, and this investigation he was putting together with my help would be a career maker for him when all was said and done. To the Feds, this was business as usual. Once a month I met with all of them to update all parties involved. They preferred to meet at this old broken down school behind Dunkin Donuts off Route 110. It was set back where no one could see us.

As Big Ray and I were using this time to build our business, the agencies involved with the investigation were working overtime trying to put the pieces together and connecting the dots. You couldn't even imagine how much legwork was required in this type of effort. First things first, the cops needed a few sales by some of these dealers to get the legal authorization to get wiretaps for the phones. Then they could legally start with video surveillance. It would ultimately be a very long process. This is where Big Ray and I came in. Big Ray would be the one who offered to make the initial buys for the DEA so they could get the ball rolling. I talked Ray into it relatively easily. The fact that the Feds would pay him each time he made a buy only sweetened the pot.

81

In the parking lot of the Ocean Crest Diner, Big Ray sat in his Mercedes awaiting Ira Kilstein's arrival. It was starting to drizzle on this late night in November. About four cars away sat Agents Weider and Hawaii in the DEA van. Though Kilstein and Big Ray weren't buddies, they did know each other well enough to do business. Kilstein was scared shit of Big Ray, and I can't say I blamed him. In fact, Big Ray's initial arrival in town is the reason I started carrying a gun. We had quickly become friends, and one thing led to another.

So now Ray sat waiting to purchase four ounces of cocaine from Kilstein, which would be directly handed over to the DEA agents. He was also wearing a wire that recorded everything. Kilstein showed up in his BMW and pulled next to Big Ray's car. He jumped out, leaned into the window, and tossed Big Ray the four ounces, took the cash, and left. Agents Weider and Hawaii stepped out of the van two minutes later. Handing over the cocaine to the Feds, Ray cracked a smile. So did they. Step one was now complete. Everything was now ready for this thing to move forward. For Big Ray this was strictly a business decision long term. He was intent on taking over all the coke business in Huntington, so the best way to do that was to eliminate the competition. It was a strategically bold move. Infamous gangster James Whitey Bulger did something very similar back in the 1970s. Ruthless, but at the same time ingenious, would be the way I would describe it.

Disaster almost struck for me, and if it hadn't been for some quick thinking I would have ended up in jail. My girlfriend Vanessa had been on a six-month binge of painkillers and cocaine. It was destroying our relationship by the day. I had really had enough. One evening when she asked me to get another eight ball of cocaine, I refused. She did not want to hear that, so she began cursing and screaming like a child. I pleaded with her to calm, down, but she only became more irate when she realized she wasn't getting her way. The more I said no, the more she wailed. The situation was now totally out of hand. Vanessa started throwing shit and broke one of the windows.

With people upstairs from us now threatening to call the police, I made a hasty decision. Thank God I did because the neighbors had already dialed 911. My safe gave me a hard time when I tried to open it, which only made things more unnerving. It was filled with thousands of pills. All at once, I grabbed the pills and three large duffle bags that had around seventy pounds of marijuana in them. I ran out the door, and Vanessa followed me outside screaming, "You're a drug dealer. Hey, he's leaving with pot everyone." The fucking nerve on her was incredible. Seconds after I pulled away from my house, four cop cars came flying up my block. That was it. I needed to get away from Vanessa for a while. I ended up moving back to my dad's while she went back to her parents.

Things had finally settled down, but I was about to be in for a rude awakening. My girlfriend was supposed to be back at her parents detoxing from the opiate painkillers. Due to the meltdown she had at our apartment weeks earlier that involved the police, I had no choice but to cut her off from them. It was for Vanessa's own good. Of course, she wasn't going to go quietly. After she made it through the first few weeks, which were always the hardest when kicking opiates, I thought things were on the up and up. Instead, the best was yet to come.

Being fairly young, neither of us could grasp the complexities of addiction and how serious it could be. Very shortly, I would find out the hard way. Cocaine and crack are hard, but opiates are a completely different type of hell on earth. They cause the user to become physically dependent, so even though someone who uses them wants to stop, the punishment from kicking the habit might be just too hard to overcome. Understanding that now, I can look back and see why Vanessa was about to do something as stupid as she was about to do.

Days later, my phone rang, and I answered in my usual pleasant tone saying, "Hello."

On the other line Vanessa said, "Hi, how are you?" Before she said anything else, I knew she was as high as a kite. Knowing her as well as I did, it was easy to detect, even on the phone. I was livid. After taking a shower, I went over to her parents' house and let myself in. Vanessa was lying down in her bedroom. Entering the room, there was a strange feeling in the air. She wouldn't look me in the eye, and it was fairly obvious why. To say she was obliterated wouldn't even begin to describe her condition. Now trying to keep her composure, she made futile attempts at a normal conversation. Her eyes rolled into the back of her head as she nodded off while in mid sentence.

I screamed, "Where the fuck did you get shit from?" While continuing to press her for info, she became unresponsive. I started to look around her room. The first place I looked was under the bed. What I found astonished me. It was fucking unbelievable.

I pulled a giant duffle bag from under her bed. Unzipping it only blew me away more. There were about fifty different large bottles of assorted various narcotics. It contained bottles of Percocet, Percodan, Vicodin, Morphine,

Codeine, Demerol, Valium, Xanax, and many more. On each bottle was the label of some pharmacy in the Huntington Village. You didn't need to be rocket scientist to figure this out. I grabbed her by the shirt and demanded an explanation. At first, she tried bullshitting me. Only after threatening her, did I get the truth. And it went something like this:

Around 8 P.M. the night before, she parked one of my cars across the street from this particular pharmacy. With a duffle bag in her hand, she bounced across the street on this stormy fall evening. She entered the drug store after making sure no customers were inside. What she did next was insane. Vanessa stepped right to the pharmacist and told her that some men across the street were holding her kid hostage, and that the child would be killed if she didn't come back with a full bag of pharmaceuticals. The pharmacist nearly collapsed from the shock of what she had just heard. Realizing someone's life might be in danger, the pharmacist asked what she wanted as far as drugs. Strangely calm, Vanessa started reading from a list she had made. Scrambling between the aisles, the pharmacist began filling the bag. When it was full, she handed the bag to Vanessa, and she left. Vanessa trotted back across the street, jumped into my car, and took off.

Absolutely dumbfounded, my ears could not believe what they were hearing. Moments later, my pager went off with a 911 after the number. It was Officer Vandenberg. Before he said anything, I knew what it was about. When I called him back, I could hear the disappointed tone in his voice. "What the hell is going on with her?" were the first words out of his mouth.

Ashamed, my reply was, "Curt, she is a total junkie."

Lucky for Vanessa, Officer Vandenberg was one of the first cops to respond to the pharmacy robbery the night before. After a few minutes of conversation, he asked, "Where are the drugs?"

I replied, "Don't worry Curt, I found them and took them."

"Good, now get rid of them," were his last words to me. After promising him I would, he then hung up the phone. Believe it or not, it would be the last time it was ever spoken about by Curt and me. Nothing ever came of it. It's like it never happened. Vandenberg passed up on an easy felony collar to protect the integrity of his investigation that I was helping him with. Vanessa couldn't have been any luckier. I had an ace in the hole with my police contacts, and it already paid big dividends for me. Officer Vandenberg really went to bat for me, and I would never forget it.

Pretty soon after the incident with Vanessa, I had a chance to reciprocate. Someone robbed a sporting goods store and stole guns and ammo. Fearing that these guns would hit the street, Vandenberg called me and asked if I heard anything about it. "Not yet," I told him but I would ask around. Talking to my pal Keith a few days later, I struck oil. Keith went on to tell me that some guy he knew from the hood was responsible. Right away, I headed home and called Officer Vandenberg. Within a week, the cops nailed the guy.

Now back to the investigation. The Feds and police had just set up a tactical operations center in a small, one level ranch on Old Country Road. It was a green and white house with a crescent shaped driveway. In that driveway, now sat a huge Winnebago with these weird looking antennas on it. On the roof of the house sat two giant circular dishes of some type. The house was now buzzing, like a beehive with activity, as agents and police began coming and going 24/7. Neighbors started to notice, but no one knew what was up.

From this residence, everything took place. By now, all the big players in this drug ring were being followed non-stop. All phones were now tapped, and the dealers' houses were being monitored by video surveillance, which was set up on telephone poles close to the homes. A lot of the customers who were buying off distributors Kilstein and Reikert were dealing out of bars, so the police began placing undercovers at these places to watch them closely. This was really very early in the investigation, so it would take a lot of this type of police work to build the case. And the hunt was just beginning. It was a target rich environment, so the police would be very busy.

In 1992, it ended up being an extremely busy year. A lot of shit was going to go down, some good and some very bad. Things started out with a bang. Big Ray, who I was now calling "Twinkie," called me and gave me a heads up on some hippie who was sitting on twenty pounds of some real good pot. He wanted to rob the guy, and asked if I wanted in. My response was, "Shit yeah." Pulling it off would be a cakewalk. The hippie lived in an apartment on the second floor of this house that was set back off the street. It had a private entrance on the side of the house that was concealed by some long green shrubs that blocked the view from the street.

That night, Big Ray called me and informed me that the hippie would be out for hours. So after picking me up, Twinkie told me the weed was in the refrigerator in the kitchen. When we got to the house, I said, "I got this. Wait here and I'll be right back, Twinkie." Big Ray waited in the car as I walked up the driveway and opened the first door to the staircase. Surprisingly, it was unlocked. I ran upstairs and kicked the apartment door off the hinges. I went inside, opened the fridge, and grabbed two good-sized bricks of pot that were inside. It totaled twenty-one pounds. I grabbed them and split. Twinkie was all smiles. We split up the weed and made ten grand a piece for five minutes' work.

There was this customer of mine named Mark, who had been a regular client since I started dealing. He was a junkie who used heroin and cocaine frequently. Mark did sell substantial amounts of weed and coke. Having a soft spot in my heart, I let him run a tab with me at times, and he was usually good about paying it back. Thanks to his girlfriend, he ended up falling into the hole with me for over $10,000. As more and more time passed by, the tab was not being paid. Then Mark came to me with an idea to try to clear his debt. He wanted to rob one of the local pharmacies after hours. "If you are crazy enough to do it, what the hell?" If he was successful doing it, I could flip the pills over and make some good money. It sounds crazy, but the movie "Drugstore Cowboy" inspired an awful lot of pharmacy robberies.

A few nights later, Mark and his girlfriend parked in back of a small drug store on Route 110 in Huntington. With a small ladder he had brought, he climbed onto the roof of the pharmacy with an ax and began smashing his way through the roof. It took him about twenty minutes. When the hole was big enough, he dropped down inside and headed straight for the cabinets. Using a crow bar, he popped open all of them. He began filling a giant green garbage bag, shoving as much as he could fit inside. After three or four minutes, he was done. He tripped the alarm and ended up smashing out the back door window and jetted. His woman drove him straight to my house. After going through the inventory, I was somewhat disappointed. The haul was so-so. I did get a few good bottles out of it though.

The summer of 1992 was a hot one, but the temperature outside paled in comparison to the heat the Feds and police brought to town. They were now everywhere. Every bar in Huntington was being staked out, and all the dealers' houses were under surveillance around the clock. The only two people who weren't being watched were Big Ray and me. While waiting patiently before making another buy for the Feds off Kilstein, something unthinkable happened. Vanessa would come close to blowing the whole damn investigation.

One night, while drunk, Vanessa started bothering me for money to get high. "Forget it," I yelled. Immediately after hearing me say no, she began making threats. Not taking her seriously, I asked her to leave.

"You'll be sorry," was the final thing she said before leaving. Being completely spiteful, she drove over to Kilstein's house and knocked on his door. What she did was incomprehensible. Answering the door, Kilstein was puzzled and asked her what she wanted. She told him that Big Ray and I were working with the police setting him and other people up.

Can you imagine the fucking nerve of her to do that? Kilstein called me a half hour later and made me aware of what happened. I was in complete disbelief and couldn't fathom the betrayal. Of course, I denied everything and went on to tell him that she was off her rocker and to pay her no mind. Thank goodness he just brushed it off and forgot about it. The next morning, I called Officer Vandenberg and informed him of what she did. It should have surprised him, but it didn't. After she robbed that pharmacy, nothing she did shocked him. She was a total loose cannon, capable of anything. We ended up having to wait another month to make a buy off of Kilstein because of what she did.

Kilstein's business kept chugging right along, and he never entertained the idea that what Vanessa told him might be true. The following weekend, while he was at a club called Coco's in the Huntington Village, he did something that angered the DEA greatly. Kilstein happened to notice he was being followed by two narcs while at this club. Being the wiseass and pompous bastard that he was, he grabbed the waitress and sent the agents a bottle of champagne. He then smiled when the waitress delivered it. Kilstein then pulled out a roll of cash that could choke a horse. While flashing the cash, he threw a $500 tip on the bar, giggled, and left. Ira Kilstein and his crew of thugs were terrorizing Huntington as bad as Adolf Hitler and his brown shirt bully boys did Germany in the early days of the Nazi party. Ira and a few of his goons once beat up a helpless waiter in a Chinese restaurant for bringing him the wrong order. He was a cancer that needed to be removed.

Heads were about to start rolling. There were about to be a bunch of big time arrests that would happen almost in succession. The first one was of a police officer named Michael Dowd. He was the boogieman, your worst fucking nightmare come true. Dowd was a cop out of the 75th Precinct on Sutter Avenue in East New York, Brooklyn. East New York was a drug-infested area that usually led the city in rape, robbery, and homicide annually. Being subjected to the depravity and insanity that working in that area brought, it ended up turning him from cop to crook. It's actually not that hard to believe, considering what was going on in those days. With so much illegal money in circulation due to the drug trade, some cops became jealous and frustrated seeing so many of these low life's cashing in while they risked their lives for a measly $600-$700 a week. It didn't seem fair, right? Some cops such as Dowd were going to take advantage of this. The New York City Police Department was far from immune from corruption. Back in 1971, a cop named Frank Serpico became the first cop to openly expose corruption to the Knapp Commission. It was the biggest example of it, that is until Michael Dowd came along. Officer Dowd started out as a good cop, but somewhere along the way things changed. By 1986, there were complaints about him robbing drug dealers and taking pay offs to look the other way. Dowd and some other crooked cops he worked with were booting in doors of drug dens and robbing them straight up. They would then sell the product they would get from these non-sanctioned raids back on the street.

These cops became so cocky they started flaunting what they were doing. Michael Dowd drove to work at the 75th Precinct in a brand new, cherry red Corvette, and would have limousines pick him up after work to take him to Atlantic City. These were your tax dollars at work. Between 1986 and 1992, Dowd lived a charmed life, but like most good things, it would come to an end. Police in Suffolk County, while monitoring some drug dealer's phone line, picked up some chatter between Dowd and the other drug dealer. They ended up arresting Dowd, and soon after everything he was involved with came to light. Dowd was making sometimes as much as $8,000 a week while working for the city. This guy was some piece of work. His arrest eventually led to the forming of the Mollen Commission, which like the Knapp Commission had done earlier, investigated police corruption. It ultimately led to more than thirty more arrests. The days of Michael Dowd sniffing cocaine off of his dashboard in his patrol car were finally over. He ended up doing more than ten years in prison.

Our buddies from the Crash and Carry Gang were the next in line to have their heads on the chopping block. Federal agents arrested fourteen of them almost simultaneously. The FBI and other law enforcement agencies had been building a case against them for years. Having been operating for over a decade, the police hadn't had much success in putting a stop to their continuing crime spree. A big break came in 1990, when a witness who saw them robbing an art gallery in SoHo in New York City, decided to follow them in his car. I don't think the witness who did this knew just how dangerous this was. Back in 1987, some guy tried doing something similar when he witnessed one of their crimes in progress. Before trying to intervene, his car was hit with a fire-bomb while he was still inside the car. Luckily, the man wasn't killed. Some of the members of the gang were cold-blooded killers.

In 1990, the gang hit two art galleries in the same neighborhood but on different days. The first was the Naham Gallery, located at 381 West Broadway in SoHo. At approximately 2 A.M., five masked bandits took bricks and shattered the gallery's front glass window. Within minutes, the gang grabbed as many as forty pieces of Roman and Etruscan artwork that dated back as far as the 3rd Century BC. They also snatched at least three paintings, all of which totaled more than a million dollars. The real break came from the second job the gang pulled.

Not long after the Naham job, the Crash and Carry Gang hit the Dyansen Gallery, located at 122 Spring Street in SoHo. Some time around 4 A.M., the gang smashed the window and grabbed over a quarter million dollars' worth of Leroy Nieman originals, put them in a stolen truck, and left. At the time, the gang didn't realize some nosy bystander who was at a deli just down the street saw them loading the truck and decided to follow them. For whatever reason, they never noticed the guy tailing them in his car. It would be a costly mistake.

The gang then parked the truck in some garage in Brooklyn, where unbeknownst to them, the man who followed them saw the place they stashed the truck and called the police. Ten minutes later, the police arrived and surrounded the garage. After entering, the cops discovered the truck and were able to recover the expensive artwork. By late October 1992, following the arrests of the gang only months earlier, the indictments came in. The ring leader, whose name was Robyn Francois, a few of his brothers, and ten more from the gang were all indicted on multiple felonies which ranged from racketeering, conspiracy to plan and commit as many as six murders, and moving stolen merchandise across state lines. Some of these subordinates such as Chris Campanella were indicted on lesser charges and only received short prison terms. In March 1994, the gavel came crashing down. Robyn Francois was convicted of most of the charges and received more than a life sentence. Some of his brothers were also convicted and received varying prison terms. The gang had been dismantled, but not completely. When Chris Campanella got out of jail, he went right back to his criminal ways and kicked it up a notch. I'll get into that in a bit.

During that summer of '92, I took a job bouncing at the Black Oak Saloon. Not really needing the money, it was more of a keep people guessing about my activities. I also was teaching karate. I needed a vacation, so I decided to visit Jake out in California. It was great to see him because it had been a year and a half since we had seen one another. When Jake picked me up at LAX Airport in Los Angeles, he was so happy to see a familiar face. We gave each other a big hug, and he took me to the beautiful Loews Hotel in Santa Monica, which was right near Venice Beach. I updated him on everything going on back home.

We spent most of our time working out and bar hopping during the evening. Bill Clinton was staying three doors down from me at the hotel. I ended up meeting Bill and found him to be a very entertaining guy who was cool as could be. Jake and I talked a lot while I was there, and I informed him that if he turned himself in, Officer Vandenberg would work out a deal for him for the pending charges back in New York. Jake didn't go for it. He just had a son born, so I guess he didn't want to be separated from his child. The police back home wanted him bad, so he had to know this would eventually catch up to him. The time flew by when I was in California, and it was now time to get back to the insanity that was going on in New York. Vacations can be refreshing. This one was just what I needed because when I got back to New York, there would be even more arrests of people I was involved with.

Landing back at JFK Airport, I began to feel ill when exiting the plane. I was coming down with a bad viral infection that just crushed me. I looked like grim death. While being driven home by my buddy Brian Bartholameau, he repeatedly had to pull over so I could vomit. It was dreadful. After arriving home, I went straight to bed and would remain there for almost two weeks. When I started to feel better, it was time to meet with Officer Vandenberg and the DEA to set up a second buy off of Kilstein.

Even though the investigation had been going on for over a year, the Feds still wanted more evidence to make their case bulletproof. Big Ray and I met them up at Jayne's Hill, which was a park that sat on the highest point on Long Island. The Feds wanted to have Big Ray have Kilstein meet him at a restaurant called The Clubhouse to make the deal. Agent Joe Weider would be sitting with Big Ray eating dinner while this went down.

So later that night, Big Ray beeped Ira Kilstein and told him to bring 9 ounces of cocaine to The Clubhouse. It was around 9 P.M. when Kilstein entered the dimly lit establishment. Big Ray and Agent Joe Weider were sitting in my usual booth, which was isolated between both bathrooms. As Kilstein sat down, Big Ray introduced Agent Weider as his boy from Brooklyn. Kilstein didn't give it a second thought. Agent Joe Weider looked the part, sporting five gold chains and a Rolex worth about 20 grand. Big Ray handed Kilstein a bag with the cash, and then Ira handed over a brown paper bag with 9 ounces of cocaine. Kilstein just made a direct sale to the DEA. He was finished.

The DEA could have nailed him right there, but they wanted to roll up his entire crew. Twinkie called me later that night to fill me in. It was crazy what we were involved with at that time. Big Ray and I were sneaking around right under the cops' noses making a fortune while working for them. Big Ray actually had the cops convinced he was working some job as a contractor in Queens, when in reality he was living in Syosset and was slowly making a push to take over everything. Our plan was awesome, and we executed it flawlessly.

My weed business was now taking off again, getting bigger and bigger. I was working with three different marijuana traffickers who were all reliable. One was a guy named Jerry Wood, who was a brother of one of my friends, and my other two dealers I mentioned earlier were Fast Frankie and Charlie Sykes. Jerry Wood was convenient because he lived about ten blocks away from me. I called him when Fast Frankie or Charlie Sykes weren't available. Things were going smoothly, but you knew it wouldn't last.

While I was busy hustling weed, Big Ray was continuously expanding his cocaine operation. He now had a Colombian national named Caesar living with him, who was from Barranquilla, Colombia. This guy was a big time cartel member who had connections for unlimited kilos of cocaine. It was a really big risk Twinkie was taking by having someone of that status living with him. Caesar was trying to expand the scope of this operation out into Suffolk County. We were all playing in the major leagues. This guy Caesar would have had Big Ray killed had he found out about our involvement with the police and Feds. But we kept everything hush-hush. The DEA agents would have lost it if they had any clue what we were up to. It was all part of the chess game we were playing.

A short time after Big Ray had made the second purchase of cocaine for the Feds off Kilstein, I decided to go back to work as a bouncer at the Black Oak Saloon. I was finally fully recovered from that nasty viral bug that crippled me. My first night back working would be an extremely memorable one for a few reasons. As I sat on my stool by the door checking IDs, I was being practically suffocated by the low hanging cloud of cigarette smoke that hovered through the entire joint. Nearly having an asthma attack, I stepped outside to get some fresh air. When I did, a guy came walking up to the door that I hadn't seen in quite some time. His name was Glenn, and he was a shady character who ran with some other crew from out East. How we ended up talking about what we did is still a mystery to this day.

Knowing that I was a major drug dealer, this guy decides to start bragging about some big deal he was doing for someone. I think he was trying to impress me. My ears couldn't believe what this idiot started telling me. He went on to explain to me that he was going to body pack almost a kilo of China white heroin, and bring it into the country of Bermuda for some Chinese gangster. The Asians now dominated the heroin trade in the New York area, and some high-ranking members in Chinatown were running it. Heroin had always been a problem in New York, but it seemed to be getting worse due to the fact that the heroin that was coming from the golden triangle was the purest smack ever to be put on the street. People were overdosing in record numbers.

This moron I was talking to in the parking lot told me everything from the day he was travelling to the airline he was using. Remembering everything this guy said word for word, I went and paged Officer Vandenberg from the pay phone in the bar, and told him I had a huge tip for him. Vandenberg was blown away at what I passed along. Immediately, he contacted the Feds and they worked out some kind of plan. Less than a week later, I received a call from Officer Vandenberg thanking me. That tip I gave him paid off huge. That guy Glenn was arrested, trying to import almost an entire kilo of smack when entering the country of Bermuda. What the Feds did was flag this guy to customs, and he was yanked off the line at the airport. He was then put in front of some x-ray machine in some back room, and that was all she wrote. His goose was cooked. Like so many before him who had disappeared in the Bermuda Triangle, this poor bastard was neither seen nor heard from again. Did I feel bad? Not really. Why he was boasting about something so serious as international drug smuggling, I have no idea. Hey, all is fair in love and war.

My night at the bar was not over, though. An hour after I talked to Vandenberg, something weird happened. While I was standing looking out the door of the bar, I felt a tongue lick the back of my neck. It sent shivers down my spine. Then while closing my eyes, I felt a finger go right up my ass. That caused me to jump up and turn around. Standing there was a ridiculously hot woman who could have been a model. She was probably in her early 40s, with dark hair and blue eyes that sparkled in the dim light. Her body was incredible. I was speechless. She then says to me, "I want you to fuck me."

Almost in disbelief, I uttered, "Sure." Something like this had never happened to me before, so it almost made me nervous. The woman, whose name was Candy, then began telling me about herself. As we talked, she started to grope me aggressively. She ripped my buttoned down shirt open and began sucking my massive chest. That was it. I told the bartender I was stepping out, and Candy and I jumped into the back seat of my Cadillac Seville. This woman rocked my world. When I exited the car a half hour later, I could barely stand. My legs were gone. What an unbelievable way to end my night. When I reentered the bar, people started cheering.

Unfortunately, only days later, I would have another close call that was way too close for comfort. And it was going to cost me a huge chunk of dough. My old pal Kip Santiago came to me with what would turn out to be a terrible idea. He was in debt to me for almost $20,000 still, thanks to him getting ripped off a while back by those guys from the Brooklyn Street gang, the Decepticons. Slowly, I let him sell some weed to work off his debt from the past year or two and got it down to about $20K. It wasn't getting cleared up fast enough, so I started pressing him for my money.

He had gotten in touch with Jake in California and came up with this idea to sell cocaine to clear his tab. This is where I came in. Santiago wanted me to use Jake's old Colombian connection in Jackson Heights so I could cop the coke. I was the money man, so without me, it wouldn't work. A year and a half earlier, I swore I would never get involved in selling cocaine again, but somehow this fucking asshole talked me into it. It would be yet another extremely costly mistake. So I contacted the guy in Queens and set up a meet with him. On my first trip, I only picked up a half kilo. After I brought it back, I gave it to Kip, and he turned it over fairly quickly. At first I didn't give it much thought, and that was my mistake. About ten days later, Santiago called me and told me he wanted another one. Like a fool, I took another trip into

Queens against my best judgment and picked up a full kilo. It cost me $27,000. The price of cocaine had nearly doubled since 1987. Multiple seizures of some huge amounts drove the prices way up.

The next night, a friend of mine spotted Kip out at a bar with a guy named Joe Joe "Sushi" Nakamura. Nakamura was a conniving little weasel who sold cocaine and heroin, and also had some lose ties to Asian organized crime. Joe Joe's parents owned a Japanese restaurant in the city, hence the nickname Sushi. When I heard this, I fucking lost it. I was supposed to meet with Kip the next morning for breakfast to give him a half-kilo, but when I heard who he was hanging out with, I almost changed my mind. I should have. Nakamura was one of Ira Kilstein's boys who Big Ray and I had already ratted out to the DEA. He was already done, so it was imperative to find out why Santiago was with him. My only fear was that Kip was dealing with this asshole.

Morning arrived, and I couldn't get to the IHOP pancake house fast enough. Vanessa and I sat at a table and ordered our breakfasts as we waited for Kip Santiago to get there. Walking in, he had this dumb ass look on his face. I said, "Sit the fuck down and wipe that stupid smile off that face." His expression turned to fear. Knowing what was at stake, I laid out everything to him about my involvement with the cops and Feds. He was shocked at what he heard. I asked him who he was dealing with and he said, "It was no one I knew." Point blank, I asked him if he was dealing with Joe Joe Nakamura. The piece of shit lied right to my face. Explaining to him how serious a problem him dealing with Sushi would be, I again asked him the same question. He swore he wasn't. I said, "Look asshole, we already gave Nakamura up to the Feds."

There was a half-kilo of coke in the trunk of my car. I didn't want to hand it over until I was sure about Nakamura because this could come back on me really badly. Even after warning him, telling him about my involvement with the cops, and admitting having served Nakamura up on a silver platter, this scumbag lied to me a third time. Like a damn fool, I took his word. Vanessa went outside to my car, grabbed the duffle bag with the coke, and put it in Kip's car. Had I known he was involved with Joe Joe Nakamura, I would never have given it to him. For me, the third time would be the charm in getting involved with Santiago. We parted ways after breakfast, and I went to go work out.

The S.O.S. would come in later that night. Around 10 P.M., Vanessa and I went to the Westbury Drive-In to see a movie. Halfway through the flick, I got a page from an unknown number with a 911 at the end of it. I was right in the middle of getting a blowjob, so it pissed me off. There wasn't a pay phone at the drive-in, so we ended up leaving the movie early. Hopping onto the Northern State Parkway, I drove for about seven minutes before pulling off the Round Swamp Road exit to use the pay phone. After dialing, I anxiously waited for whomever it was to answer. It was Kip Santiago's father who picked up. "Ahh, fuck," I knew it. His dad relayed to me that Kip was busted in Nassau County for sale of cocaine. I only asked his father one question and that was with whom he was arrested. "Joe Joe Nakamura," was his reply. I dropped the phone and punched my hand through my windshield. As blood spurted every-where, I raced back to my house.

The news couldn't have been any worse. My mind was in overdrive won-dering just how bad this was. And let me tell you, it was really bad. It turns out that this was the third felony sale Joe Joe Nakamura made to the cops. This time it was for a half kilo of coke. The cops had been working him for some time, and that douche bag Santiago was the one who supplied him with it. Nakamura, Santiago, and some hapless buffoon named Paul Aronsen, who unfortunately was dumb enough to give them a ride, were all arrested and were now in huge trouble. Nassau County is the absolute worst place in the State of New York to get into trouble. They were super-intolerant when it came to drugs and handed out extremely long jail sentences for narcotics trafficking.

During the trip back to my house, I could only assume the worst. Nearly hyperventilating, I realized I had another half-kilo of cocaine in my room. When I pulled up in front of my father's house, I expected the cops to already be there. Thank God for me, they weren't. I ran inside, went straight to my safe, and opened it. Without any hesitation, I grabbed the half-kilo and flushed the shit down the toilet. I did not yet know the extent of the situation, but I didn't want to take any chances. All I could find out about the charges was from his brother. Time suddenly went by agonizingly slow. Kip's father and brother went to his arraignment the next day and returned to tell me Kip was being held on $10,000 bail. That was shockingly low for someone who had just been charged with major felonies.

I know what that meant, and that was that the cops flipped him. One thing was certain, he would never have the balls to rat on me because he knew I would put him and his family in the grave in a New York second. Kip's brother collected enough money within a week or so and bailed him out of the Nassau County jail. I met with Kip the day he came home and noticed he had a black eye. Some big black guy kicked his ass and took his sneakers when he was on the inside. When I met Kip, the first thing I did was check him for a wire. His word was meaningless, and I would never trust him again. I ripped him a new ass and cursed him out for ten minutes. The fact that he lied to me about Joe Joe Nakamura was my biggest gripe. Kip wept like a little baby. "Man the fuck up," I told him after slapping the shit out of him. Now sobbing, he asked what he could do. At the top of my lungs, I screamed, "You are lucky I don't kill your ass, you motherfucker!"

After talking about an hour, we came to an agreement that I would leave him alone for the time being and let his court case shake out. He would then have to repay all of my money. How much was that? Well, he owed me $17,000 for weed. Add another $27,000 for the coke that went up in smoke thanks to his betrayal, and the grand total was $44,000. I was so fucking enraged I seriously considered killing the fuck. Forty-four thousand dollars is a lot of money, but for the time being I had to forget about it. There was still my business to run. To sum things up, Santiago never did a day in jail. Less than a year later he quietly packed up in the middle of the night and went into hiding. That motherfucker moved out of state and never returned. To this day I haven't been paid. I should have killed that piece of shit when I had the chance. Ahh, regrets, there is nothing like them.

And still there would be more bad news. As if the shit with Santiago wasn't enough. Marijuana dealers were a much lower priority as far as law enforcement went, but for some reason the DEA was going to make a major push to shut the pipeline down. They were going to go after the big traffickers, which meant my connections. The first domino to fall was my friend's brother, Jerry Wood. Jerry had just told me that he had a load coming into New York in two days. I was supposed to see him on Friday, but that would never happen.

That is because that Thursday, Jerry went somewhere in Nassau County to pick up a car that was loaded down with hundreds of pounds of pot that had just arrived from Arizona. Unfortunately for him, when he got inside the car, he wouldn't get far. He had barely gotten the car into drive when dozens of DEA agents pounced on him. They boxed his car in, ripped him out, and slammed him down on the street. Jerry was confused, and I'm sure very distraught. After he was cuffed, he was brought to the DEA's office in the Huntington Quadrangle. He must have agreed to cooperate because he was home the next day. I ran into him that Friday afternoon about two blocks from his house. Pale and extremely shaken, he told me what had happened. What was interesting was that Agent Joe Weider was the one who arrested him. Had the Feds let Jerry drive away, they would have run into me shortly after because some of that load was going to me. Sometimes you are just damn lucky.

The second domino to fall with my weed connects was Charlie Sykes. Sykes was a major trafficker, and I only did things with him about a half dozen times. He was responsible for a good portion of marijuana that ended up on the streets here on Long Island. Charlie Sykes started calling me here in New York from Tucson, Arizona, to tell me he was going to be in town with a big load. We must have talked a good seven or eight times over a two-week period. Seeing that Jerry Wood had just been arrested, I figured the timing was perfect because all my customers needed weed. All I needed to do now was wait. Before Sykes came to town, I received a call from Big Ray who demanded from me to get to his apartment right away because it was an emergency. He sounded really serious, so I went straight to Twinkie's crib. What he told me was incredible.

Twinkie explained to me that he had just met with Agents Joe Weider and Bob Hawaii. What they told him was downright scary. They informed him that Charlie Sykes was coming to New York with a 2,000-pound load of marijuana. Sykes was already under investigation in Arizona and now the DEA in New York was going to try to take him down here. The agents asked Ray if he knew where or when this was going down. Agent Weider also told Twinkie that Sykes was moving 1,500 kilos of pot a month out of Tucson. Charlie had major buyers in Los Angeles, Vegas, Boston, and New York. The Feds hated him and wanted him gone. Big Ray played dumb and gave the agents nothing. He did, however, come right to me and spill the beans. Big Ray knew I worked with Sykes on occasion, so he wanted me to watch my ass. I knew Fast Frankie was going to get some of that load so I called him and explained everything that I heard. I even told Fast Frankie about my involvement with the DEA. He thought it was a great idea, me working with the Feds, and thought it was a smart move that could benefit us all. I cut my involvement with Sykes right there because I didn't need to get caught up in some federal sting.

Some time that following weekend, I got a page on my beeper from Fast Frankie. Not wanting to take any chances, I drove a good ten minutes from my house to return his call. When I did, he informed me that the weed was in. As unbelievable as it was, Charlie Sykes managed to sneak nearly a ton of marijuana in right under the DEA's watchful eyes. How he did it while under surveillance is something I still wonder about. Fast Frankie was now living in Long Beach, which is a seaside town on the South Shore. He had quite the set up there. Frankie's house was a beautiful two-story condominium right on the beach. I drove down there the day after Fast Frankie and I spoke. With me was a briefcase with over 100 grand in it. Pulling into Fast Frankie's driveway, I was stunned at how gorgeous the place was. The building was brand new, and his backyard went out onto the beach and the Atlantic Ocean.

After giving me the grand tour, we got down to business. He instructed me to pull my car into his garage. Once I did, he closed the garage door behind me. I stepped out of the car, and Frankie asked me to follow him into this back room in the back of the garage. There was over 1,000 pounds of marijuana in it. He asked me how much I wanted. I responded by saying, "I'll take 300, if that's okay with you."

"Right on," said Frankie. We both started loading bricks of the pot, which weighed 40-50 pounds each, into the trunk of my Cadillac. There wasn't enough space in the trunk, so I had to put the rest on my back seat. I didn't have all the cash, so I told Frankie I would settle up with him later in the week. The weed was wrapped up in Saran wrap with Charlie Sykes' trademark Mickey Mouse contact paper covering the outside. I bid Fast Frankie farewell, he opened the garage door, and I left. The ride home would be anything but uneventful.

Driving back to Huntington, my pager went off with a 911 and the number. It was Officer Vandenberg. I again pulled over at the Round Swamp Road exit on the Northern State Parkway to return his call. He said he needed to meet me right away at the abandoned school behind Route 110. Hesitating momentarily, I reluctantly agreed to do it. I had over 300 pounds of pot in my car, so I was taking a huge risk meeting him. I trusted my gut and did it anyway. The afternoon was bright, and there was a strong wind blowing.

Pulling into the school parking lot, I suddenly became very tense. Standing there with Officer Vandenberg was DEA Agent Joe Weider. My stomach instantly got all knotted up. I pulled up to them, parked my car, and hopped out. With a shit-eating grin on my face, I greeted them with a, "What up?" as we shook hands. Curt Vandenberg was his usual friendly self, but Agent Weider was stone faced. Without him having said anything, I knew he was pissed off about something. As Vandenberg and I were speaking, Agent Weider rudely interrupted and said he had some issue he wanted to talk to me about.

He then explained to me that he had been investigating some huge weed traf-ficker named Charlie Sykes and that my name came up. Right after he said that, he reached into his back pocket and pulled out about ten pieces of paper. With an angry red face, he pointed out my father's phone number in about seven different places on the paper. "I don't like the fact that we have this guy Sykes' phone tapped, and your phone number is all over it," said Agent Weider. He began to threaten me.

Thank God Officer Vandenberg intervened on my behalf because I was going to snap back at the agent. Curt said, "Hey Joe, settle down and talk civ-ilized to him." After all, I was doing some huge things for them. Reminding Agent Weider about the heroin bust I gave them, I asked him what he wanted from me. What happened next raised my pucker factor. Agent Weider sud-denly jumped up and took a seat on the trunk of my Cadillac. Having 300 pounds of marijuana right under the DEA agent's ass, I became unnerved. Things got sort of hazy with my vision. It felt as if I were about to have an anxiety attack. Luckily, he didn't smell the weed. Now knowing I was dealing with Charlie Sykes, Agent Weider asked me if I could buy 100 pounds of pot off of Sykes for them. "Why me?" I asked.

He said, "Because it's the right thing to do. You are now working for Team America." Yeah, it may be the right thing for you, but definitely not for Sykes.

"No thanks," was my answer. He then tried bribing me by offering me $10,000 in cash if I would do it. "Hmm," then, "No," I again responded. Agent Weider looked as if he wanted to strangle me right there. I tried to tell him that Charlie Sykes was a friend, someone I knew, and that I didn't have a reason to destroy his life. Our conversation ended, right there.

Both Agent Weider and Officer Vandenberg said goodbye and left. I fi-nally exhaled, got in my car, and left. Holy shit. That could have been a fucking disaster. What's crazy, is right after I saw the Feds, Charlie Sykes was busted less than a month later. The DEA got one of Sykes' long time friends who was also a customer of his to roll over on him. The guy ended up buying 500 pounds for the Feds. Sykes was now on his way to federal prison for a long time. Fast Frankie would be the next to fall, just not yet.

We were now well into November 1992. The investigation had been going on for over eighteen months. On Sunday, November 26th, I woke up extremely excited because I was going with my man "Cake" to see my beloved Kansas City Chiefs play the New York Jets at the Meadowlands. It was a very cold and windy day with an overcast sky. We even had some snow flurries. I hadn't seen Cake in a long time. We knew each other since school and had worked together when I was eighteen at some tree company. Cake was another sick bastard. One day while working at the tree company, Cake took the bucket truck up to thirty feet, hung his ass over the side, and took a shit. It missed the boss by only a few feet. That was one of the many pranks Cake pulled when we worked together.

When we got to the Meadowlands, it was a madhouse. People were all dressed in green and going crazy. After partying for a while, we went inside and took our seats. The game was fairly close until the third quarter, when something terrible happened. While Cake was at the concession stand getting food, a defensive end on the Jets named Dennis Byrd, took an awkward hit and fell motionless to the ground. We didn't know it at the time, but Byrd was paralyzed from the neck down. When the game resumed, the Chiefs pulled away and won the game. During the trip home, Cake and I had a long talk. I knew he hung out with Ira Kilstein once in a while, but I didn't know he was holding onto large amounts of cocaine for him. Hearing that, I warned him to back off his involvement with Ira immediately. But it was already too late. His fate was already sealed. That bothered the shit out of me because I never wanted to see any of my friends get arrested with Kilstein. Some of my pals were told by me to stay away from him and the reason why.

Sunday, December 6, 1992, was D-day for the operation with the Feds and police, with 5 o'clock A.M. as H hour. As most of us slept that night, no one could have imagined what would be taking place all over town by the time anyone had awakened. In the pre-dawn darkness, the police, and Feds started kicking in people's doors with search and arrest warrants. Ira Kilstein's door was the first to go down. About thirty members of a joint task force, consisting of the DEA, the state police and the local police smashed down Kilstein's door at exactly 5 in the morning. Ira Kilstein was just going to sleep when they entered his residence. Ira immediately grabbed more than a kilo of cocaine and made a mad dash for the bathroom. The entire place was mirrored from floor to ceiling, so the Feds had some trouble finding him initially. Agent Joe Weider intercepted Kilstein just as he had begun to flush the product. Agent Weider maced the shit out of Ira because he tenaciously resisted arrest. The Feds then gave Kilstein quite a beating. Most of the others who were arrested went quietly and did not try to resist.

When I woke around 10 o'clock in the morning, I received a call from Big Ray who told me to put on News 12. I did just that and was absolutely smitten with what I was seeing. Kilstein's arrest, along with the rest of his cohorts, was the top news story. Reality had just set in, and it suddenly dawned on me just how serious everything we had been involved with was. There was a huge perp walk that showed everyone who was arrested, all donning government issued silver bracelets and shackles being moved from a bus into state police headquarters. I called everyone I knew and passed along the news. We were all singing ding-dong the witch is dead. This was truly a moment to savor. People all over town couldn't believe what went down. Tragically, my man Cake was one of the people arrested. Another three or four idiots who I warned to stay away from Kilstein were also locked up in the sweep. I couldn't believe that they were so fucking stupid. Well, after Santiago betrayed me and did the same shit months earlier, it shouldn't have surprised me.

My masterpiece, which I had put into motion nearly twenty months earlier, had finally come to fruition. I didn't realize the magnitude of what was happening until I started seeing it all over the TV. All the networks were now running the story. Liaisons from the New York State Police had stood at the podium and given the rundown as to what officially transpired. And that was that almost thirty people from mostly the town of Huntington were arrested in what was a combined effort by federal, state, and local law enforcement. It was one of the biggest drug sweeps ever done on Long Island. The tally was impressive. Not only were 28 people arrested, there were also a lot of drugs and cash confiscated. More than two kilos of cocaine was discovered during the searches. A substantial amount of marijuana was also found. Over two dozen guns were taken off the street. Having the Feds on board also enabled the cops to seize more than twenty luxury vehicles along with three houses, Kilstein's being one of them. Early the next day, the story of the bust hit all the papers. Officer Vandenberg made sure all the news stations and papers got the story. It was his way of shoving it up Kilstein's ass as a parting gift. The New York Times ran with a headline that read, "28 Suspects in Suffolk Drug Ring Arrested."

Later that same day, Big Ray and I went to my father's house and paged Officer Vandenberg. About five minutes after beeping him, he called back. I said, "Congratulations Curt."

He said, "Thanks," and went on to tell me how none of this could have happened without us.

Although I realized that, I replied by saying, "Thank you," but stressed the fact that this was his show, and he deserved all the accolades that were now coming his way. As I said earlier, Curt Vandenberg was an impressive man, and it took a lot of effort and perseverance to put this kind of thing together. Twinkie and I told Vandenberg that we would meet up with him when things settled down a bit.

Hungry from all the excitement, both Big Ray and I went to The Clubhouse for a celebratory dinner. Just as Kilstein had done when Jake was busted, Twinkie and I would celebrate his misfortune. We dined on Chateau Briand for two, and both enjoyed lobster on the side. Staying for nearly two hours, we rejoiced at what we had done. I looked at Big Ray and said, "Hey, you fuck with the bull, you get the horns." That was the last thing I said before we left. My attitude may sound awfully callous, but I mentioned before you had to be cold and somewhat ruthless in this business if you wanted to survive.

During the aftermath of the big bust, there was a tremendous amount of chaos and confusion. One thing became clear, however, and that was that nobody wanted to go to jail. People were pointing fingers at each other so fast it would make your head spin. Most of the poor saps who were arrested were middle class, white, and soft. Except for a few, many of them had never seen the inside of a jail cell. And suddenly only one thing mattered and that was saving their own ass. Before anyone was done being processed, twenty-six out of the twenty-eight suspects had already signed statements on Kilstein and agreed to further cooperate with the police in the future. Was it surprising? Hell no, it wasn't. A lot of times even hardened criminals will cave in under the pressure of facing heavy jail time.

Within days, some of the people who were arrested had by now made bail. The main guys in Kilstein's organization were being held on very high bail, so the majority of them would remain in the county jail in Riverhead until their cases were done as far as the legal process went. My buddy Cake was being held on a quarter million dollars bail. Lucky for him, his parents were eventually able to put up their house to get him out so he could fight the charges from home. For some reason, Cake decided to be a stand-up guy and refused to cooperate with the District Attorney. That was a colossal mistake on his part. Every other person who was arrested in the sweep rolled over like some circus animal. As far as Kilstein went, he was finished. With twenty-six of twenty-eight defendants all agreeing to testify against him, his future looked bleak.

Kilstein had lost the most by far as material things went. His million-dollar house was the costliest, but he also had all of his prized possessions taken. And that was $70,000 BMW, a $60,000 Mercedes, a $110,000 Mustang, and a Scarab racing boat that he kept in Huntington Harbor. I didn't feel sorry for him in the slightest because had he had his way, I would have been busted two years earlier with Jake. The ploy that Big Ray and I pulled off to eliminate the competition was carried out to perfection. Some may even call what we did expedient.

Following the arrests, Huntington had turned into a ghost town virtually over night. Not a soul was in sight. It's like someone turned on the lights and all the cockroaches scattered. For a while, most of the bars in town were empty and for good reason. People were running scared and any of the remaining dealers with half a brain would take some time off and lay low. Thanks to the major operation, Officer Curt Vandenberg would earn his gold shield. He was promoted to Detective and would now wear a suit and tie to work. First he was moved to the burglary unit. After a few years, he was promoted to homicide and would go on to have a long and distinguished career. Curt was a great cop who always was smart enough to see the big picture. Big Ray and I were two people he would never forget. We helped fast track his career. Curt always looked out for us. Now as far as the DEA agents Weider and Hawaii went, they would lock our asses up in a fucking heartbeat even after all we had done for them. So for now, Big Ray and I had to proceed with caution.

As the weeks started to go by, I slowly began picking up the pace with my weed business. But I did it on the down low. My only major connect left for the pot was Fast Frankie. I didn't know it at the time, but his days were also numbered. The Feds had been working overtime trying to rid New York of all the major weed traffickers. One morning, I grabbed the paper and was pretty surprised with an article in it. There was a story of a massive marijuana bust that went down only a mile from my house. Some Chinese guy named Eldon Chan and his son were caught getting a delivery of 1,200 pounds of pot that had come in from Galveston, Texas. The DEA tracked the load from Texas to Huntington. Agents Weider and Hawaii were in on the arrests. They made sure to call Big Ray and I to boast of their victory. In a half joking half serious manner, Agent Weider said to me, "You're next."

I replied by saying, "Catch me if you can, I'm the Gingerbread Man." Big Ray took a great deal of pleasure in the cat and mouse game with these G-men.

His sense of humor was more on the perverse side and living on the edge had become part of his personality.

Thinking back, it was Big Ray's signature when he used to rob people, that was downright bizarre. After he was done tying up his victims and then robbing them, he would go on to take a shit on the living room floor next to where the people were tied up. That blew my mind the first time I heard it. He was without a doubt one of the craziest son of a bitches I ever had the pleasure of knowing.

Big Ray wasted no time in stepping in and filling the void with most of the coke dealers having been arrested in the sweep. By now, a lot of the remaining people who weren't caught up in the sting needed cocaine. And he was right there to capitalize on the situation. It was a smart move on his part. Twinkie's business quadrupled in no time. Officer Vandenberg was now out of the picture, being caught up in his new role as Detective in the Second Precinct, but the DEA were still in Huntington in force. That fact didn't seem to bother Big Ray one bit.

One night while Twinkie was at his apartment, he noticed the DEA surveillance van sitting directly across the street from his crib in the parking lot of this ice cream store. They were watching him. So very quietly, Big Ray snuck out his back door and hopped his fence. He then doubled back and came up behind the van. While the agents stared at Twinkie's apartment, Big Ray opened the back door to the van and jumped in. Big Ray said, "What up, bitches?"

Agent Weider just looked at Twinkie and said, "Hey, fat boy."

Twinkie, while laughing hysterically, asked them, "Is this the best you got?"

Bob Hawaii replied by saying, "We were in your neighborhood and decided to check up on you." After a few moments of insults being thrown back and forth, Big Ray jumped out, mooned them, and went home. He called me and told me what happened. It didn't surprise me at all. Remember, we were always thinking three or four moves ahead of them. We knew Vandenberg would never turn on us, but I anticipated that the DEA would do it the first chance they got. And they did not disappoint. Shit, we knew them better than they knew themselves.

Law enforcement had done a fairly good job of dismantling the criminal organization we had been involved in since 1985. But it was far from thorough. Their impatience had let quite a bit of the quarry to slip through the trap. The biggest score for the Feds was nailing the Crash and Carry Gang. They were by far the biggest thorn in the side of the FBI. Most of them were in jail by now. Some of the top leaders in the gang would never see the light of day, while others would be out of jail within a year or two. And the ones who did get out went right back to a life of crime. Shutting down Jake was another win-win for the cops. His house was a hub for all kinds of illegal activity. But they did make the mistake of not reeling in Big Ray and me when they had the chance. And they would pay dearly for that. Between Twinkie and me, we continued to flood South Huntington with a continuous supply of cocaine and marijuana.

We just finished a two-year run of basically being able to deal drugs with police protection. Our involvement with them and setting up that huge bust allowed us to operate while they looked the other way. It may sound crazy, but it's true. Had you told me back in 1985 that seven years later I would still be dealing, only acting as a double agent by being a federal informant, I would have said you were nuts. But that is the insanity of this lifestyle. If you weren't smart enough to roll with the changing times, you would have the life expectancy of a housefly.

I finally got back into a groove working out. Twice a week, I would meet up with Master Barathy to try to stay sharp with my martial arts training. Things just weren't the same without my training partner Jake around. He was the perfect training partner, big, fast, and tough as nails. Before the cops raided Jake's house, we had planned on opening a new American Combat Karate school with Master Barathy. It regrettably never got to happen. For the last two years, I was also working out with my buddy Keith, who was an excellent amateur boxer. My hands became lethal between the karate and the boxing. So at least for the time being, I kept a steady routine. Making money was fun, but working out was my passion. It is the one thing that kept me grounded throughout this long roller coaster ride that was my life. I even got Vanessa to go to the gym with me, which is something I should have done years earlier. After going to rehab, she really settled back down. Things were again stable for the first time in ages. There was some serenity back in my life. Again, it wouldn't last long. Having dealt drugs as long as I have taught me one thing, and that was to expect the unexpected. The unexpected always seemed to happen at the most inopportune times.

There had been so many arrests in such a short period of time you needed a scorecard to keep track. An awful lot of people I knew were among them, and it wasn't over with. One more arrest was looming on the horizon, and it would have a tremendous impact on my future and me. Being smart could carry you a long way in this business, but you also needed some luck. For Fast Frankie, the only luck he would have in that late week in March was all bad.

When I got up on the morning of March 20, 1993, I went to the diner on Jericho Turnpike to have breakfast. From there, I used the pay phone to page Fast Frankie to see what was up with the pot situation. I was now out of product, and my customers were pestering me for more. When Frankie called me back, he asked me to come down to Long Beach to have dinner with him so we could talk things over. We decided to meet at some beachfront café that he frequented.

Arriving at the restaurant around 4:30 P.M., I walked inside and the place looked empty. When you first entered the establishment, you had to walk through a bar area before heading into the back where the tables and chairs were. Sitting in the back all by his lonesome was Fast Frankie. He was in an exceptionally good mood when I got there. The waitress came over and took our order while we started chatting about business. Fast Frankie started telling me that he had a huge load coming in within a week, and that he was going to load me up. Before we even got our food, his mood would go from one of joy to one of horror.

Less than ten minutes into the conversation, a strange man walked into the back area where we were sitting and just stopped and gave Frankie and me this death stare. The man looked to be in his 50s. His haircut was regulation short, and he was sporting this navy blue windbreaker with dark khaki pants. There was also a recognizable bulge underneath one side of his jacket. He smelled like a federal agent. Fast Frankie nearly choked after seeing this. Right after the man left, I turned to Frankie and said, "That is not a good sign." By now, I could spot a cop or a Fed a mile away. Having worked closely with the Feds for two years, I could sense when something wasn't right. So believe me when I tell you, something was not right with this picture. I warned Fast Frankie that he better watch his ass, because everything I had just seen spelled trouble. Frankie, then in his best reassuring voice told me, "All is good" and not to worry. I knew better, though. When we finished dinner, Fast Frankie said he would call me when the load came in. We said goodbye, and I left. The whole ride home I kept telling myself that there was a reason that guy exposed himself to us in the restaurant. With everything that had gone on recently, I didn't believe in coincidences.

On March 26, which was less than a week since I had seen Fast Frankie, I received a call that passed along some bad news. My bouncer friend Sean McGuire called me to tell me that a friend of his, who was working in the Philadelphia area called him after reading a story in a newspaper called "The Trentonian." The headline was, "Dog Finds 1.2 million of Pot in Truck." Well as it turns out the article was about my man Fast Frankie. It came as no surprise at all. This was life in the hustle game. Between speaking to my friend Sean and then calling Officer Vandenberg, everything was confirmed. The picture became very clear, and the story goes something like this:

Sometime during the afternoon of March 24, a truck with Arizona license plates was travelling east on I-78 in Union Township New Jersey. Some curious state trooper saw the driver commit some minor infraction and pulled the truck over. For one reason or another, the state trooper decided to have the truck towed to headquarters for further inspection. It was there where the Jersey trooper detected the odor of marijuana coming from some food containers in the back of the truck bed. They then brought in the drug-sniffing dogs to confirm their suspicions. After that, it was a wrap. Upon searching the truck thoroughly, the cops discovered 700 pounds of marijuana. Both drivers who were residences of Phoenix, Arizona, were placed under arrest on the spot.

The drivers both agreed to cooperate and hand over who the pot was destined for, and that was my man Fast Frankie. The cops had one of the drivers call Frankie and explain to him that the truck had broken down, and that they needed Frankie to come to South Jersey with a van so he could get his load. Fast Frankie fell for it hook, line, and sinker. About six hours later, Frankie pulled into some truck stop not far from state police headquarters in New Jersey. He was like a lamb being led to the slaughter. Minutes later, the state police surrounded the van. Arrested were Frankie and some poor schmuck who decided to take the ride with him. This was about as bad as bad could get for Frankie, because New Jersey has really strict drug laws. Miraculously, Fast Frankie was out of jail within days. That usually meant one thing, and after everything you read up to this point, I'm sure you can connect the dots. Most people in these situations usually tucked and rolled. Strangely, had it not been for Sean McGuire's friend spotting that article, I would have been a sitting duck.

About two days after finding out about what happened to Fast Frankie, I got a page on my beeper. The code that was punched in after the number was

Frankie's. My throat became very dry after seeing who it was. A few minutes later, I took my car and drove a short distance to a pay phone to return his call. When Frankie answered the phone, he said, "Hey, what's up?" as if everything was fine.

I immediately responded by saying, "I heard about what happened."

For thirty seconds things went quiet. His silence was deafening. Then he responded, by saying, "You heard about that?"

"You bet your ass I did," I told him. All of a sudden he began acting strange. I owed him a few thousand dollars from our last deal, and he asked me about it. Refusing to acknowledge what he was saying, I told him to come to Huntington if he wanted to talk. I assumed he flipped for the cops, so I wasn't going to let him record me admitting to anything.

The day after, he pages me from the pay phone from the IHOP restaurant in Huntington. Foolishly, I agreed to meet him there to talk. As soon as I pulled into the parking lot, I spotted some guy sitting alone in his car right next to Fast Frankie's car. Just outside the parking lot, I also noticed two more vehicles with middle-aged white men in each one. I realized what was going on, so I told Fast Frankie to follow me in his car. The reason I did that is I wanted to see if those other cars would follow. And lo and behold, they did just that. After about five minutes, I gave them all the slip. That was the last time I ever saw Fast Frankie.

Enough was enough. I had run the gauntlet for the last eight years and came out relatively unscathed. But there had been too many near misses. By now, almost everyone I had been involved with was in jail. I could feel the noose tightening ever so slowly around my neck. The long arm of the law had made a point of taking out many of the key players in our organization. But in the overall picture, it accomplished very little. Drugs were still pouring in, so trying to stop it would be comparable to trying to empty the ocean with a teaspoon. It was definitely time to shut down for the time being and reanalyze the situation. I didn't have much of a choice being that all of my weed connections were in prison. My God, the last eight years of my life were nothing short of incredible. Looking back, it's almost impossible to believe everything that had gone on. Had I not lived to see it, I wouldn't have believed it either.

In April, Vanessa and I took a trip up to Mystic, Connecticut, just to get away to decompress and have a change of scenery. It was exactly what was needed at that time. Things were really getting great between Vanessa and me again, and it made me realize why I fell in love with her in the first place. Now clean and sober, she started to glow again. She was gorgeous when she wasn't getting high. We had such a great time that I never wanted to go home. I felt like a new man by the time our trip was over.

After returning home from the trip, I almost went underground. My mom was managing some hotel off the Long Island Expressway in Plainview, so I had her rent me a room in her name for the next month. The next thing I did was rent a car. My main objective for the time being was to stay out of Huntington. So for the next month, Vanessa and I took a local vacation, staying at the hotel and eating room service. During this time, I tried to come up with a solution for my problems with finding another weed connect. When I first started dealing years ago, I never wanted to become some kingpin. I wanted to be just big enough to make a great living without taking that step up. Now things had changed, so I didn't really have a lot of options. And a former childhood friend of mine would be the answer to my prayers.

While running around Huntington one day, I ran into an old pal who I hadn't seen in about ten years. His name was Darren, and we used to ride BMX when we were kids. Darren was a laid back, really down to earth, mellow guy so he was easy to get along with. It turns out he was home on vacation. He now lived in Tucson, Arizona, and had just graduated from college there. Shortly after we began talking, he said he knew a lot of key players in the marijuana trade down in Tucson. My eyes lit up like a slot machine. Darren was in a rush, so we made plans to talk the next day.

Darren and I met for lunch that Thursday at an Italian restaurant in Commack called Emilio's. The food was outstanding. Most of our conversation revolved around business. Darren was home for the summer, but the real reason for his stay was he was already engaged in some weed smuggling from Tucson. He had some customers in Manhattan who he had been mailing boxes of marijuana to on a regular basis. And soon he would start doing the same for me. Things looked like they would work out after all. Within two weeks, I got my first package in the mail. It was thirty pounds of pot. As great as this was, I needed much bigger amounts than they wanted to do by mail. Darren then explained to me that if I came down to Tucson, he could get me whatever I needed and that the price would drop significantly. So for the rest of the summer, we sort of just did the smaller amounts to keep my customer rolling along. The plan was to wait until fall and then go to Arizona and start buying down there. It was a step I had hoped to avoid, but there really wasn't much of a choice. The remainder of the summer was uneventful except for one thing that stood out to me.

Big Ray's coke business was steadily increasing, and he was really enjoying his success. Some time in July, one of his buddies from Syosset came to him saying that two guys he knew who were cocaine dealers and also stockbrokers needed a couple of kilos of blow. Big Ray said sure, he would take care of them. What the two soon to be unsuspecting victims didn't know was that Twinkie had other plans for them. The guy who was the middleman set everything up. When the two stockbrokers arrived at some parking lot to do the deal on that hot, muggy July night, I'm sure the last thing on their mind was getting rolled. But that is exactly what would happen.

Twinkie stole a car and then headed over to meet the marks in the Town of Jericho. He turned into the parking lot and spotted their Mercedes on the far side. Big Ray pulled right next to them, got out, and jumped into the backseat of the Mercedes. After shaking hands, Big Ray pulled out a .45 caliber pistol and said, "Don't you fucking move." The two brokers froze and started begging for their lives. As cool as Twinkie was, he could be downright ruthless. "Where's the money?" demanded Big Ray.

With tears dribbling down their faces, the driver says, "It's in the trunk."

Big Ray duck taped both of their hands behind their backs. He took the keys out of the ignition, got out, and opened the trunk. In it, was a duffle bag with nearly $60,000 inside. Once he grabbed it, he would leave a token of his appreciation. Before leaving, Big Ray hopped back into the back seat of the Mercedes, pulled down his Fila sweatpants, and took a huge, 18-inch steaming shit on the backseat. "It was a pleasure doing business with you," was the last thing Twinkie said. I couldn't stop laughing when he told me the story the next day.

In late August, as the summer began setting, Big Ray would give us all another really good chuckle. Ira Kilstein was still in jail, being held on a million dollar bail. Kilstein's wife, however, was not. She was released after agreeing to cooperate with the District Attorney following her arrest. And it wouldn't take long for her true colors to shine through. Rene, which was the name of Kilstein's wife, was a major party girl, another cocaine queen. She drank daily and did cocaine almost every night.

Being out only days after her arrest, she began fucking half the town. Anyone with half a brain could have seen this coming. Having a monster cocaine habit, it was only natural for Rene to gravitate toward whoever was the big man on the cocaine scene. That now was my friend Big Ray. Ray was hanging out one night at the West Hills Inn, which was a local bar. In comes Rene, sucking up to him. After maybe two drinks, Big Ray had Kilstein's wife in his car, sucking his dick. When she finished, Big Ray took her to his apartment and fucked the shit out of her. He literally had her sniffing cocaine right off his erect penis. His intent was basically to degrade her as best he could. The next day, Big Ray made sure to tell everyone. Days later, it got back to Ira Kilstein, who was by now losing his mind in jail, hearing about the things his loyal wife was doing. Talk about pouring salt in the wound. Not only was Big Ray responsible for getting Kilstein busted, he also nailed his wife. It was the icing on the cake. Agent Weider and Officer Vandenberg took Twinkie out to dinner when they found out what he had done. Kilstein's stay in jail was a horror show. He was blinded in one of his eyes after someone stabbed him in it and then threw bleach in it.

It was once again time for a major change in my life. Before I could start going down to Arizona to start my own hustle there, I had to move. There was way too much heat around town to stay in Huntington. So as the winds of autumn started coming in during October, I packed up shop and moved into Manhattan, the Upper East Side to be exact. My bouncer friend Sean McGuire knew some real estate broker who got me a great deal on a duplex, which was also a penthouse. It was right near the corner of 78th Street and First Avenue. The price was somewhat reasonable, costing $4,000 a month. For that neighborhood, it was actually a pretty good deal. Sean, my buddy, decided to move in with me, along with Vanessa, my girlfriend. My bedroom was on the top floor, which went out on to the roof. The place had an incredible view, looking out toward the East River. Sean took the downstairs bedroom. We had a fireplace in the living room, and boy would that come in handy because the winters of '93 and '94 were brutal. I bought all new furniture when I moved in. We were now living large. But it would cost a small fortune, costing me $1,600 a month just to park my cars. Living in the Big Apple was definitely a unique experience I really would enjoy.

There are times in life when everything seems to go right, and then there are times when nothing but bad happens to everyone you know. As I was getting acclimated to life in the big city, I would receive some terrible news that would shake me up pretty bad. One day while out in Long Island, a call came to Vanessa's parents' house for me. It was one of my customer's Mark's girl-friend. Mark was the guy who robbed that pharmacy in Huntington to clear his debt. Both Mark and his girl Chrissie were now living on 77th and Central Park West. He was still doing some small business with me so that first month living in Manhattan I saw him quite a bit. I happened to be in front of Vanessa's parents' house the afternoon we got the call from Chrissie. As Vanessa was walking down the steps to hand me the phone, there were tears rolling down her cheeks. Damn it, I knew this was going to be bad. Almost afraid to answer the phone, I finally said, "Hello."

The first thing Chrissie said was, "Mark is dead." My breathing stopped, and I was speechless momentarily.

Finally after regaining my composure, I asked, "How?" She told me he died from a heroin overdose the previous evening. Remember when I mentioned how potent the Asian heroin was? Well, it ended up taking my man Mark out. The heroin Mark injected was responsible for a huge spike in recent overdoses that had killed dozens in the tri-state area. What a damn shame. Mark, who was only 24 years old, was a gentle soul who would be missed. His final resting place would be the lonely and desolate potter's field.

Unfortunately, it wouldn't be the last of the bad news that week. Five days after Mark passed away, I got another phone call passing along even more disturbing news. This time it was my sister calling. She explained to me that a former customer of mine named Craig had also died. His story was indeed horrific. Craig was smoking crack for two straight days, when he decided to head to Brooklyn to get some heroin to bring himself down. After snorting a bag of the same China white that killed Mark only days earlier, he began driving home on the Long Island Expressway back to Huntington. Not long after his return trip began, Craig overdosed and passed out behind the wheel of his Chevy Malibu. Unconscious, he swerved off the highway and drove right underneath an 18-wheeler on the side of the road. He was decapitated instantly. It was a gruesome way to go out. That was life in the fast lane. These stories were far from unordinary when you live in that lifestyle. In New York, people died every day from drugs.

By December it was really cold in New York, and we had already been hit with multiple snowstorms. My friend Darren finally called me and gave me the green light to come to Arizona for some business. Within 24 hours, I was in the air on a Southwest Airlines 747 bound for Tucson. Darren picked me up at the airport and took me back to his house. The scenery was beyond description. There was sand in every shade of brown imaginable and cacti everywhere. It was a landscape of which I had never seen except on TV. After checking out Darren's house, I had him drop me off at the Hotel Park Tucson. I was tired from the travelling and wanted to get some rest. Darren and I made plans for the next day.

Waking up the next morning, I was ready to roll. My buddy Darren picked me up at 11 A.M. to go get lunch. He took me to this Mexican restaurant that was off the hook. After we ate, we had to go to some house to meet the pot connect. It was in some neighborhood where all the houses were really small with tile roofs. We ended up waiting a good hour before our hookup arrived. Around 1:30 P.M., two tall brothers walked in the door. They were both Mexican and in their late 20s. I had $50,000 buy money sitting in Darren's truck. Following the introductions, we got right to it. The two brothers, whose names were Dan and Hector, then asked us to take a ride. Not giving it a second thought, Darren and I followed them in their champagne colored Mercedes all the way across town.

They ended up pulling into this huge trailer park where there were hundreds of trailers that were sitting in rows. Most of them were over 50 feet long. As we made our way through the maze, we stopped at one trailer that looked no different than any of the others. Dan and Hector got out and motioned for us to come over to them. They unlocked the lock on the door and cautiously unlatched and opened them up. Inside, the whole thing was filled with marijuana. It was an awesome sight. Before Fast Frankie got busted, he told me it was easier to get 40 pounds of pot in Tucson than it was to get $40 worth back in New York, and he was right. Tucson, Arizona, and El Paso, Texas, were the two most drug filled cities in the country. The brothers started showing me different bails, asking me what I wanted. There were many grades available. Darren had already set up a ride to transport my weed back to New York. I told the Mexican named Dan that I had $50,000 on me. They offered to send me 300 pounds. I jumped all over it. The $50k would be a deposit for the load. Carefully inspecting the merchandise, I picked out about eight different bails that were all light green and stunk like a Christmas tree. The weight came out to 320 pounds.

My boy Darren was going to take care of wrapping and arranging everything from here on out. Dan and Hector took their time counting the money.

When they were through, we all headed to a titty bar for a few drinks. The set up Darren had was near perfect. His drivers were an old couple in their 70s from Tennessee who drove a sheriff's vehicle. At the time, state troopers weren't as inclined to pull over senior citizens, especially ones in a law enforcement vehicle. Mine was not the only load that would be on the truck. They were making at least two other stops on the way. One stop was in Ohio, and the other was in Washington, D.C. We set it up like this, after my pot arrived in New York, one of the Mexicans would fly to meet me in New York to collect the rest of his money. Things were good to go. I spent my last few days in Arizona either riding dirt bikes with Darren or getting drunk at the strip clubs. A lot of the drug dealing in Tucson took place in those titty bars.

Heading back to New York on the plane, I started running the whole scenario in my head. As much as I trusted Darren, I was still taking a huge gamble. If the truck got nailed when driving cross-country, I'd be out 50 grand. When I landed back in New York City, it was like a frozen tundra. Snow and ice were covering everything. I had just spent a week in picture perfect, 70-degree weather while in Arizona so the cold bothered me more than usual. Entering my apartment, Vanessa was there to welcome me. She was ripped on Percocet. That totally annoyed the shit out of me. Now cognizant of the fact that she was up to her old tricks, it didn't sit well with me. I had a good size load of marijuana on its way, and the last thing I needed was her getting into trouble or bringing any unwanted attention my way. But it was already a forgone conclusion. She was off and running once again, and there would be no stopping her. Much to my dismay, there was little I could do about it.

The day my load of pot arrived was a strange one. Early in the afternoon, I received a page on my beeper from Darren. I was busy eating lunch in Little Italy at Umberto's Clam Bar with Vanessa. The fried calamari and baked clams were downright delectable. After finishing lunch, I returned Darren's call and found out the drivers were in town with my smoke. Wasting no time, Vanessa and I got into my black Thunderbird and started hauling ass back to my apartment. Darren told me the drivers would meet me at the Howard Johnson my mother worked at on Long Island. It was a smart idea, but I had to drop Vanessa off first. Normally, I would have taken First Avenue uptown, only there was construction on it that would have really bogged me down. Instead, I decided to take Park Avenue. While racing to beat the red lights up in the East 60s, I almost had a near catastrophe. I was about to blow a red light when three people started to cross Park Avenue. Jamming on my brakes, my car started skidding to a stop. The pedestrians never looked before crossing the street. As my car went slightly over the line, my bumper just nicked one of them. The man turned and put both of his hands on my hood. It was the actor Woody Allen who I almost had run over. Jesus Christ, was that close. I was totally embarrassed. Feeling like an idiot, I apologized to Mr. Allen and he smiled and said, "It's okay." A few minutes later, I dropped Vanessa off.

There wasn't much traffic when I left the city for Long Island. It only took me about thirty minutes to get to the hotel. My mother was working when I got there. Going through the parking lot, I spotted the sheriff's vehicle that Darren's drivers were in. I pulled up right next to them, got out and said, "Hello." The old man opened the back hatch on the truck, and we began transferring the large bags with the pot from his vehicle to mine. As soon as we were done, the old couple couldn't get out of there quickly enough.

Spotting what appeared to be a few undercover cars, I said, "Oh shit." I pulled my car out and wasn't sure what to do, so I drove away. Maybe I was just being paranoid, but I wasn't taking any chances. I drove through the adjoining neighborhood for a few minutes and then drove back to the hotel and stopped at the main entrance. My mother cracked a warm smile when she saw me come into the hotel. Completely unaware of what was going on, she was surprised when I asked her for a favor. I asked her if she would let me stash some luggage in her office. She reluctantly agreed. I then grabbed one of those push carts the bellhops use to transport suitcases and loaded it up. After placing all eight bags on the cart, I wheeled it to the manager's office. Once inside, my mom came in and rolled her eyes at me. My mother said, "Patrick, what have you gotten me into?"

"Relax," I said. "I'll get it out of here in a little while." She returned to work. I can't believe I put my mother in that type of potentially compromising situation. Later that night I returned and got my load of marijuana out of there. My poor mother was, let's just say, quite angry with me.

Before heading back to my apartment around midnight, I stopped at my father's house and grabbed $175,000 from one of my safes that I kept at his house. Had I been pulled over on my way back to the city, I would have been screwed royally having all that money and drugs on me. When I got back to my crib on East 78th Street, I cautiously made five separate trips from my car to the apartment. I just dumped all the pot on my living room floor and went upstairs to bed. Hector, the Mexican I was now dealing with in Arizona, would be arriving the following afternoon to collect his dough.

I picked Hector up from LaGuardia Airport around 2 P.M. Before going to my apartment, we went to Angelo's Italian Restaurant on Mulberry Street. Hector was blown away by how great the food was. "Only the best for mi amigo," I told him. Lunch was followed up by a stop at Ferrara's for some delicious pastries. It was then time to get down to business. Hector and I got back to my apartment and sat down on my long black leather couch. I pulled out his money and he began counting it. No more than five minutes later, there was a loud knock at my door. "Who is it?" I asked.

"It's the police," barked an annoyed sounding voice from the opposite side of the door.

"Oh God, not now," I said to myself. "Just a minute," I told them. I ran upstairs and grabbed my blanket from my bed and threw it over the eight bails of marijuana only a few feet from my door. Hector was speechless. He threw the cash back in the duffle bag. I slowly took a deep breath and opened the door, and stepped into the hallway closing the door behind me. You could smell the weed all the way in the hallway. "What can I help you with, Officers?" I asked them.

The cops pulled out a sketch of what was clearly my girlfriend Vanessa. They asked me if I had seen this woman or if I knew where she might live. I told them I had no idea and that she definitely didn't live in this building. It happens that the week I was in Arizona, Vanessa was going around to different doctors' offices in the area stealing prescription pads, forging them, and then filling them. Lucky for Hector and me, the cops left two minutes later. Thanks to Vanessa, I could have been busted. Thank the Lord, I wasn't. I couldn't believe she nearly blew everything up on me the first time I had the Mexicans in town. That night before Hector returned to Arizona, I took him to a club called The Vault. It was one of New York City's most famous sex clubs. People walked around the place half naked wearing dog collars, leather chaps, and had sex right out in the open. Hector was mesmerized and had never seen anything like it. When we left the club, I grabbed Hector an issue of Screw Magazine, and he called a transvestite prostitute who I had banged a year earlier. He ended his trip with quite a bang, and after nailing the transvestite, I think he was in love.

I kept running my business as I had been, which was get a load of weed, hook up all my customers with enough to hold them for a while, and lay low for a bit. Then when the time was right, I would do it again. I did this five or six times a year. The pot business wasn't twenty-four hours a day, seven days a week like the cocaine business was. The money wasn't as good, but it was still very profitable. During the next six months, things went smoothly. I had four more deliveries from my connect in Arizona during that time span. But again, it wouldn't last. By July, Hector and Dan were in jail along with the old couple they used as their drivers. Someone in Ohio set them all up. In the fall of 1994, I went back down to Tucson, and Darren hooked me up with a new connection. This time, I used my own drivers, who were friends of mine from Huntington. I paid them $10,000 each time they made the trip. My new connect was a white guy named Brad. I don't think that was even his real name. Brad was a major player in the Tucson drug-dealing scene, and he was part-nered up with some big time members of a Mexican drug cartel.

My two years living in the city were definitely wild ones. I was living like a rock star, and every other night was an adventure. But while I was living lifestyles of the rich and shameless, my old pal Jake, who was on the run from law enforcement as a fugitive, was living under an alias and moving around trying not to stay in one place too long. He was constantly looking over his shoulder, and what made things even more difficult was that he now had a family to provide for. Big Ray Scalzo completely controlled the cocaine busi-ness in Huntington now, but he could feel the walls closing in. It was only a matter of time before his number finally came up. You want to hear the music; you have to pay the fiddler. Karma was eventually going to catch up with all of us, and believe me, one way or the other, we would all get our just desserts.

In June, I received a page on my beeper while I was getting a massage with a happy ending in some Chinese bathhouse on the Upper East Side of Man-hattan. It was Detective Curt Vandenberg. When I called him back, he said we needed to meet in person and that it was extremely urgent. A slight chill went through me before I agreed to meet him at the old school off Route 110 where we used to meet. My mind began drifting, trying to figure what the rea-son could be. When I arrived at the parking lot as I had done quite often in the past, I was disappointed to see Agent Joe Weider with Detective Vanden-berg. As usual, he looked really pissed off. After exchanging greetings, they got right to it. Agent Weider asked me if I knew about something big that had gone down about a week earlier. I said, "What thing?"

He scowled and looked at the ground in disgust. "We don't have time for these fucking games of yours," barked Agent Weider. He must have assumed I was being cagey, but I honestly did not know what they were talking about. A little while after leaving and giving them nothing, I did some investigating, and this is what I found out.

The prior week, there was an armed robbery in Nassau County. While an armored car showed up at some business to either pick up or deliver a substantial amount of money, masked men, who were heavily armed surprised the guards and took them hostage. While being held at gunpoint, the guards watched as the thieves robbed the truck. At some point during the robbery, something went tragically wrong. One of the guards heroically tried to take action and stop the rip off. He ended up being shot and killed in the struggle. The masked bandits made off in some stolen SUV they used as a get-away car, with over $100,000. When the thieves dumped the SUV, they torched the vehicle. The whole thing started to make sense to me now. It reeked of Chris Campanella's work. Those guys were crazy enough to pull a job like that. That's why the DEA and Detective Vandenberg pulled me in to ask me about it. They figured I might know something.

But I hadn't seen Chris in over four years. We hadn't been in touch in a long time, and now I was awfully glad that I had not seen him in ages. The robbery was big news, and the police and the FBI would hunt tirelessly to bring the killers to justice. It would take fourteen years, two more murders, and a lucky DNA hit to unravel the mystery. Whether you are a thief or a drug dealer, you better remember this, when you start dropping bodies, you are going to get the law's undivided attention and become their number one priority. Once that happens, you might as well reserve yourself a cell in prison because it's only going to end one way.

By 1995, my girlfriend Vanessa had been locked up for stealing prescription pads and prescription forgery at least five times. Each and every time it happened, I would end up spending a huge chunk of dough on lawyers and fines to keep her out of jail. It was a total waste of time and money because she wasn't getting the message. She was completely addicted to painkillers and had been for years now. There was no light at the end of the tunnel as far as this went. When the summer started that year, she had already spent three of her six-month stay in a rehab upstate and still had three more months to go. I admit with all the chaos she brought to the relationship, I missed her tremendously. So when August rolled around, it was time to pick her up. Driving up the Taconic Parkway to get her, I thought a lot about what I could do to support her. But there isn't a lot you can do to help a junkie when they don't want to help themselves. After I picked her up from rehab, we grabbed a hotel in town for a few days. Port Jervis was a beautiful town. We ate out and saw the sights. What I didn't know was that by the time we left to go home, I got her pregnant. Things were again about to change drastically.

A month and a half later, we found out the news about the bambino. We were both very excited. Business for me had changed recently. I was still in the same line of work, just the delivery system was different. My weed connection in Arizona, Brad, now had his own airplane. I'm not talking about some two-seat Cessna. This plane was good-sized. The first few times I met the pilot, we would meet at some hotel in Dubuque, Iowa. They would load my rental van up with weed, and I would drive it back halfway across the country.

The leaves on the trees on Long Island were now changing as we entered the fall of '95. Vanessa and I were sharing a house we rented in the affluent section of Cold Spring Hills. She was due to give birth some time in April, and it was a crazy time trying to prepare for everything. We left the city because we wanted to be closer to our families when the baby arrived. During those nine months, Vanessa started spending money like it grew on trees. Now I made great money, but you have to be careful with your spending or it would eventually catch up with you. I was thinking of hanging up my spurs and quitting the life of crime. With the due date getting closer, I wanted to do a few more loads and then just disappear from the scene. Easier said than done, and you just knew it wasn't going to be that easy.

In December, I met the pilot at a small Republic Airport in Teterboro, New Jersey. It was one of those airports that handled many smaller in-country flights. I walked through the airport with barely any security and out on to the runway where Brad's plane sat in the damp, chilly evening air. The pilot and his wife were both smiling at me when they saw me. "How was your flight?" I asked them.

The pilot's wife replied by saying, "It was like a bucking bronco coming into the New York area." Everyone was at ease because this was about the sixth time we had done this.

Earlier that week, I spoke to Brad in Arizona, who told me he was throwing something else in my load and to see what I could do with it. That something Brad was talking about throwing in was a half-kilo of pure heroin. "No way," I told him. I believed in karma and didn't want the type of trouble it would bring. It turned out that Brad not only sold large amounts of marijuana, he also sold kilos of heroin and cocaine. I was only one stop on this mystery tour, and the pilot had at least three more stops on the Eastern seaboard, so they were in a hurry to take off. I helped the pilot unload my weed, and we put it on this cart that helped carry luggage. The pilot's wife waited with the plane while the pilot and I wheeled my pot toward the small building that was the airport. As we entered the airport, we passed some rent a cop security guard who was sitting on his ass drinking coffee. He smiled at us as we rolled 400 pounds of marijuana right by him. Remember this was way before September 11, 2001, so security measures were quite different.

After loading up my van, we said goodbye, and I took off. It would be the last we would see of each other. Unaware of the terrible fate that awaited him, the pilot lifted off into the night sky and headed to a rendezvous with a federal task force. DEA agents swarmed him when he landed on his final stop on the East Coast. They nailed him with about 300 pounds of weed, and about twenty to thirty kilos of cocaine and heroin. See ya! That was the harsh reality of this business. Here today, gone tomorrow. The Feds wrangled Brad by his neck and hauled his ass off to jail after the pilot sang Requiem for a drug dealer named Brad. I was so damn lucky I didn't get caught up in that. That was my final cue to exit stage left.

Karma was something I really believed in quite strongly. And the karma train was getting ready to make multiple stops my way. After getting home with my load of marijuana, I stashed it with a friend of mine who was usually very trustworthy. But this time, this bozo wouldn't listen to me. I was adamant about keeping my pot in a dry place. A lot of the time we would use these large refrigerators to store it to keep it fresh. Only this time, we didn't have access to them. So this moron put the load on his basement floor and un-wrapped the weed. As my luck would have it, a few days later, we got a huge storm that flooded his basement. Two weeks after the storm, I dropped by his house to grab some bud. When we went downstairs, I almost had a heart attack. There was two feet of water in the basement. The majority of the pot was ruined. I couldn't fucking believe it. It was a huge loss I had no choice but to swallow. With my daughter arriving very soon, I decided to shut every-thing down.

In April of 1996, I was blessed with a blonde haired, blue-eyed, healthy baby girl. Her arrival changed my life dramatically. It forced me to look at life differently and made me understand that I was now responsible for a life. I spent 24 hours a day with her and loved every minute of it. While I was playing Super Dad, my daughter's mother, Vanessa, suffered a major relapse. Vanessa was clean and sober for six months before she became pregnant and stayed sober during her pregnancy, that was until she gave birth. As soon as the doctors gave Vanessa a shot of Demerol for the C-section, it jumpstarted the monster that dwelled deep within her. A dormant beast was unleashed that would never be corralled again. Two days after she was released from the hospital, Vanessa started doctor hopping. Doctor hopping is when someone bounces from doctor to doctor to get the meds they need, in this case painkillers. When the doctors stopped prescribing to her, she stole their prescription pads and wrote them out herself. I couldn't believe this shit was happening all over again. As each day passed, her using picked up momentum, and you could see she was heading for a major fall. Six weeks after giving birth, Vanessa pulled out of our driveway in our brand new Jeep Cherokee. When she turned off of our block, she was stopped and arrested by detectives from Nassau County Narcotics.

Vanessa called home four hours later and explained to me what happened. My emotions got the best of me, and I fucking went off on her. Once I vented my anger and frustration, I calmed down and told her to be strong and not to worry because I would handle it. Vanessa's parents went to her arraignment, and when they got back, they passed along the crippling news. She was being charged with eight felonies in Nassau County, two As, two Bs, three Ds and an E felony. Her bail was a quarter million dollars. This presented quite the dilemma. I had the money to bail her out, but I couldn't go into court with a briefcase with $250k in cash. So I hired one of my old criminal attorneys who charged me $10,000. He did nothing. He failed miserably, unable to even get a bail reduction. The Nassau County District Attorney made a plea offer and said he would not go any lower than fifteen years. Realizing how dire the situation was, I decided to hire a shark. I was referred to a lawyer who was a former Chief of Narcotics in Nassau County. Thanks to someone I knew who knew him, I got a bargain, hiring him for $60,000. The next day I dropped off a $10,000 deposit. That Friday, the lawyer filed and got a new bail hearing. The judge reduced the bail from a quarter million to $10,000. Vanessa was home later that night after I posted her bail. There were stipulations attached to Vanessa's release on bail, the biggest being that she entered a halfway house and enrolled in drug treatment. That was fine with me because she needed it in the worst way. So while Vanessa began treatment, I had the responsibility of caring for our daughter full time. Vanessa's parents helped me out a great deal, which made things more manageable. You know there are clues to people's personalities that show in their behavior if you look closely. So it really should have come as no surprise what would happen next.

Months later, as I was wrapped up in my fatherly duties at home, Vanessa was busy hooking up with some guy at her Narcotics Anonymous meetings. That was the thanks I got for saving her from going to prison for fifteen years. I spent nearly $70,000, and how does she repay me? By coming home eight months later knocked up by some thirteen-stepper. Once again, my mind could not fathom the betrayal. But that is what junkies do. She may have come home clean, but she never changed her behavior. Shame on me for being that damn stupid and letting myself fall in love with someone who had the types of problems she had. You could almost chalk it up to karma. Vanessa and I, after ten years, were now finished as a couple.

Tragedy struck in October, when my karate instructor Master Richie Barathy passed away from heart disease. Master Barathy had been a mentor and father figure to me the past eleven years. I was closer to him than I was to my own father. It completely devastated me. He was a constant stabilizing force in my life and really helped keep me in line. His passing would be the single event that would start to unravel me. Never again would I have someone to talk to or lean on when things were going wrong.

Between the load of weed I lost, Vanessa's lawyer, and the constant spending, I would burn through nearly 600 grand before 1996 was over. Luckily, I still had quite a bit stashed away. It doesn't matter how much money you have, if you are not making money but continually spending it, it will eventually run out. Although Vanessa and I were no longer together, she always found ways to bleed me for money. The baby was always her excuse. Being the nice guy that I was, it was hard to say no, and she knew it.

Time began passing by slowly. Life was now much simpler in a lot of ways. Deep down, a part of me missed the excitement, though. For eleven years, my life was constant cloak and dagger that fueled my adrenaline. And now it was gone. Sometime during 1997, I decided to try one more run for a load of weed. I went back down to Tucson and used one of my old contacts. I ended up getting about 200 pounds and was going to do it old school, mailing them back. What a bad idea. When Darren and I finished wrapping it all up, we mailed it out of five different shipping locations. Would you believe not one fucking package made it to its designated drop stops? They must have been confiscated. Again, I was out a shit load of money. These losses were taking their toll big time, but hey, at least I wasn't in jail.

Later that year, I foolishly made one final attempt to make some money. A friend of mine named Justin Mannix and I would drive out to Arizona and bring back a load of weed. I left my buddy Justin at Darren's house in Phoenix, while Darren and I drove two hours to Tucson to cop some bud. Darren started to get high, smoking the rock at some friend's house of his while we were waiting around. He began bugging out and got super paranoid. When the call finally came to go make the buy, Darren was so high that he chickened out. I ended up driving almost to the Mexican border by myself to meet someone I didn't know and had never met. The house I went to was out in the middle of nowhere in the desert. This Mexican guy named David let me in. Entering his basement, I was shocked back to reality awfully fast when I looked around and saw nearly a dozen Mexican gang bangers, all sitting around with guns. I tried to swallow, but couldn't. Under my jacket was a bag with about 70 grand in it. They could have just killed me on the spot and buried me in the desert, and no one would have ever known. But they didn't, thank God. David ended up being mad cool. Within the hour, my trunk was loaded with nearly 100 pounds of marijuana in it, and the quality of weed was awesome.

Now came the hard part. I had to still get back to Tucson to get Darren, then drive to Phoenix at 2 A.M. with New York plates, on one of the most heavily monitored roads by police in the country, I-10. By the time I picked up Darren, he was cracked out of his mind. After smoking the rock the past three hours, he was beaming hard. The whole ride home, Darren's jaw swung back and forth like some squirrel with his mouth full of nuts. Somehow by the grace of God, we made it back to Phoenix. Shortly after waking up the following morning, Darren and I wrapped up the weed and got it ready for transport. I would be flying back to New York later that day. My buddy, Justin Mannix, would be the one driving the load back east. Mannix was going to leave the next morning at dawn. I asked him to check in with me each day at 6 P.M. eastern time, to let me know all was good. Being back now two full days, I still hadn't heard from him. I began to get a bad feeling. Then, that afternoon, I received a collect call from the Navajo County Jail in Arizona. Ahh, fuck, I knew it. Yes indeed, Justin got busted. He was pulled over on I-40 right after getting on it. After talking to Justin, I assured him I would get him an attorney and to sit tight. His mother bailed him out a week later. In the end, nothing ever came of it as far as jail time for Justin. They let him off with a $5,000 fine. I, on the other hand, took another financial beating. The signs were all pointing one way, and that was to retire from the drug trade.

The opportunity of a lifetime came my way in April 1998. My buddy Darren in Arizona, was friends with a guy who played for the Kansas City Chiefs. Darren told this pro football player about me and my martial arts' training and ideas. The player ended up calling me, and asked me if I could come to Kansas City to train him for a week. Being a die-hard Chiefs fan, my answer was a resounding, hell yes. I could barely contain my excitement. When I arrived in Kansas City the next week, it felt like I was in some heavenly dream. For the sake of anonymity, I will call the player I will train Bill. Bill and I hit it off right away, and he took me everywhere with him. We worked out a total of four times that week. I turned Bill onto some of the techniques I learned from the late Master Richie Barathy, and it really opened his eyes.

In my duffle bag, I brought a bottle of Hycodan cough syrup, which is an opiate cough medicine. I was just getting over bronchitis, so it came in handy. When Bill saw me taking a swig of it, he asked me if he could take a little. I said, "Go for it, man." Bill was a big fan of the opiates and took them pretty regularly due to the injuries he would get playing football. This was something we definitely had in common. The day before I was leaving, Bill took me to a medical facility somewhere in Kansas City. The entire Chiefs football team was there getting physicals. Bill bought me a white leather football that was specifically made for autographs. We went inside, and one by one, I got to meet all the players on the Chiefs, and they all autographed my football. The experience was mind blowing, and it was one of my greatest achievements in life.

Bill, the defensive end on the Kansas City Chiefs, called me again in the middle of that summer. He asked me if I wanted to come visit him at the training camp, which was held in River Falls, Wisconsin. I had actually been there once before, going up by myself in 1996. I said yes. So I grabbed a friend of mine, whose name was Jimmy, my pet wolf Kisimo, and the three of us left Huntington on the first of August and began the long drive to River Falls. With me, I brought a few bottles of painkillers at Bill's request. I had a sealed bottle with a thousand Vicodin, a sealed bottle with a thousand Morphine tablets, and another sealed bottle with a thousand Percocet. Bill told me that a few of the other players would take all of them off my hands for top dollar. Sweet.

Jimmy, the wolf, and I checked into a hotel in the town of Eau Claire, Wisconsin. It was about thirty minutes from the Chiefs training camp. After arriving, we called Bill and let him know we were in town. That afternoon, we drove over and watched the Chiefs scrimmage the Saints and their Heisman winning running back, Ricky Williams. When the scrimmage was over, Bill came over to us and said hello. We made plans to meet up that night at the only bar and grill in town. Jimmy and I went back to our hotel to freshen up and would link up with some of the Chiefs at 7:30 P.M.

When we entered the bar and grill, I could spot Bill and some of the Chiefs a mile away. Standing at 6 foot 5 inches, 295 pounds, Bill was kind of hard to miss. With him were four other members of the team. These boys were hardcore and could party with the best of them. Bill introduced Jimmy and me to everyone, and we began an epic night of partying. After a few drinks, we got down to business. Bill, one of the other players who shall be nameless, and I stepped outside and hopped into my Jeep. I pulled out a bag that contained the three bottles of painkillers that I brought. "What do you want?" I asked the defensive tackle.

"I'll take all of them," he shot back at me. He took the entire bag for $6,000. I made a quick four grand. Bill's teammate jumped out with a smile and dumped the bag in his own car.

Once the deal was finalized, we headed back inside the restaurant and began slamming beers and shots. The defensive tackle then came back inside and started handing out Percocet to everyone. Jimmy and I popped a few Percocets ourselves, and the onslaught of drinking began. It was incredible the amount of alcohol these boys consumed. About an hour later, a few of us excused ourselves and went to the men's room. Inside the bathroom, one of the players pulled out some cocaine, and we all began doing bumps. Here I was, drinking and doing drugs with some of my idols in the sports world. This was truly a once in a lifetime evening I would never forget. My mind reached an almost perfect state of nirvana.

There was one major drawback to the trip. By the time we were leaving to drive home, I started feeling ill. I'm talking flu-like symptoms. But I wasn't really sick. Not yet realizing it, my body picked up a habit. It was to the Percocet I was taking all week like candy. On the drive home, I popped a few more Percocet and like a miracle, I felt dynamite. So I just kept swallowing more pills and didn't give it much thought.

Addiction is a complex medical issue that involves not just the body but the brain, too. It is like a time bomb that can be lurking inside anyone, and it can go off at any time. Someone could do a drug about twenty times and not become addicted, but for some reason maybe the twenty-first time is the unlucky number. Explaining it in detail is way above my pay grade. I do now know that it is the ultimate gamble, so you should really avoid doing drugs at all. For now, I was hooked pretty bad on the painkillers and didn't realize it would eventually engulf my entire life. I was about to step into a deep dark hole that took the life of almost anyone who dared to enter.

Part III

To Hell and Back

I t's only fitting that the final part of this book focuses on opiate addiction. In the present day, our country and the rest of the world for that matter is being overrun with the worst heroin and painkiller epidemic in history. It is everywhere. For decades, heroin was a problem mostly in the inner city ghettos and would sometimes find its way out to the suburbs. Now the neighborhoods of every community are flooded with it. People from all walks of life are falling victim to this now acceptable and deadly game of Russian Roulette. Your first try could be your last, and with record overdoses, you would think people would be more cautious and afraid, but strangely that is not the case. Due to heroin's ever increasing potency, it can be snorted or smoked rather than mainlining it.

The painkiller craze of the 1990s opened the door for the spike in heroin use. The federal government, sometime near the turn of the millennium, started cracking down on doctors' abilities to overprescribe opiates, which made it much harder for addicts to keep conning doctors to get their fix. This would start what is known as the sausage effect. Now with so many people addicted and no way to continue getting their prescriptions, it was only natural for these addicts to make the switch to heroin. When the government squeezed the one end, the problem just popped out on the other side. There are now all these opiate and heroin task forces all over the country trying to combat the problem. But it is a near futile effort, and no one appears to have an answer.

The painful truth is no one seemed to care when heroin was devastating the inner city minority neighborhoods. Now that Little Johnny and Suzy from the bourgeoisie started dying, people finally started taking notice. That is politics for you.

For years, my fellow criminals and I cashed in on the suffering and unquenchable desire of a population that demanded drugs. It was almost like taking candy from a baby, it was so easy. But now the universe was about to flip the script and teach me a punishing lesson, you reap what you sow.

My addiction to the painkillers would now begin a downward spiral that brought me deeper into the abyss. Very quickly, I went from taking two to three Percocet a day and in no time was taking up to twenty daily. No longer did I have anyone robbing pharmacies for me so the habit became expensive, and they were much harder to get. My money was disappearing, and I didn't seem to care. The only thing I started to care about was getting high. As long as I had my pills, I was able to function. When I would run out of them is when the problems began. Being dope sick is no joke. You become violently ill with unbearable flu-like symptoms. For about a year, there was a steady decline in my control of the situation. Who am I kidding? I lost control the minute I was physically hooked. The more time passed, the more I unraveled. And now I was about to fall off of a cliff.

It was now around 1999, and things were about to get ultra serious. Unable to get any painkillers, I started to go into horrible withdrawal. I was sick for at least three days and was far from finished kicking. Thankfully, my buddy Keith the amateur boxer came by. He immediately noticed how sick I was. He mentioned that his brother Dean was out here from the Boogie Down Bronx and was selling heroin. Normally, I would have tried to avoid that with all costs, but I was so sick I couldn't pass it up. Keith and I drove to his brother's new crib, and after introducing us, I bought two bags of dope, which cost me twenty bucks. Quickly, I dumped out a bag of smack on the table and snorted it. Two or three minutes later, my whole body became comfortably warm with euphoria. The heroin was much stronger than the pills and yet substantially cheaper. I turned to Keith's brother and said, "Give me ten bundles." The cost was $900. Heroin usually sold for $100 a bundle.

Being a Type A personality, my drive helped me become a phenomenal martial artist, guitar player and even a successful drug dealer. But now that same drive was going to work against me in a negative way. With no girlfriend anymore, heroin became the new love of my life. It was a total obsession for me. My habit became enormous overnight. Within a few weeks, I was sniffing twenty bags or two bundles a day. This continued for about three months until Keith's brother Dean just up and disappeared. Now unable to get it, I began to panic. Withdrawal began creeping in and I was miserable. Some girl I knew recommended I go to detox, so I took her advice and made some calls.

A little less than 24 hours later, I was checked into a hospital in Kings Park. Walking through those doors, I was shot to shit. Every bone in my body ached and my nose and eyes were running like a faucet. Two hours later, a nurse gave me 40 milligrams of methadone, and within about twenty minutes, my symptoms started to subside. The doctor did a slow taper with the methadone weaning me off slowly. The week in the hospital flew by and by the time I was ready to leave I was starting to feel much better. While I was in there, I met this clown named Jason who was also kicking dope. He was quite a character. Before I left, I made the mistake of giving him my number and address, a really dumbass move.

Initially, when I left the hospital, I had every intention of staying clean, but less than a week later my doorbell would ring and it would impact my life in a profound way. It was Jason from the hospital. He said he had some dope and wanted to know if I wanted to get high. Of course, I said yes. Jason used heroin intravenously. Up to that point, I had never shot up, so like a follower I let him talk me into it. For some junkies, shooting up becomes this intimate ritual they covet almost as much as the high itself. I became intrigued when Jason pulled out a kit with a bunch of needles and this rubber strap that was used to tie off. "You got a spoon?" asked Jason.

"Yes sir," I excitedly answered. After heating the dope in a spoon with some water, he threw the cotton from a q-tip in the spoon and drew the heroin into the syringe. Tightly tying my upper arm with the rubber strap, the veins in my massive forearms began bulging out. Slightly nervous, I said, "Hey, this better not kill me."

"Relax," he said.

Pink Floyd's song "On the Run" came on my stereo as Jason pierced my skin with a three cc syringe. Once the needle entered my ropelike vein, a small drop of blood trickled into the barrel. Slowly, my pal pulled back on the plunger and a powerful stream of blood filled the syringe. He then pushed the plunger and emptied it into my forearm, and then untied the strap. Instantaneously, I felt a warm itch that rapidly travelled up my arm until it hit my brain. Within seconds, the Diacetylmorphine, otherwise known as heroin, had thoroughly saturated my opiate receptors. As a strange taste enveloped the glands in my throat, I nearly shit myself. My body was overcome with a feeling of warmth and well-being that was so completely overwhelming I thought I was in heaven. Every cell in my body was now tingling with a euphoria that could only be understood by someone who had done it. Leaning back, I closed my eyes for a few seconds and was in disbelief at how high I was. Between the music and the warm rush, it had truly felt like I was in paradise. My eyelids became as heavy as sewer covers while everything slowed down to match my state of mind. I began drifting into a dreamy, semi-conscious half sleep known as "the nod." Wow, anything this good had to come with a steep price. In the blink of an eye, the devil had just captured my soul, and from that moment on I could think of only one thing…heroin.

Day by day, my money was evaporating quicker than a small puddle of water in the Sahara Desert. I hadn't made any real money since 1996. My father asked me if I wanted to take the basement apartment at his house, so I jumped all over it. The only smart thing I did in what seemed like forever was ask Vanessa's parents if they would take my daughter for the time being until I got my shit together. I was really struggling with drugs, and I explained that to them. They were really shocked when I told them about this because all the time they had known me, I was so disciplined and rarely ever got high.

Now back at my father's house, my addiction reached a fever pitch. Heroin had sucked me in like the worst riptide the ocean has ever produced. It pulled me to and fro violently and always let me know who was in charge. Within a month, I was so strung out I had become unrecognizable. My old buddy Cake, who was now home from prison, introduced me to this guy named Nelson who he had done time with upstate. Nelson was in a gang called The Netas, and he had great dope for very good prices. Some of my friends had also started getting heavy into smack. It would be the absolute darkest time of our lives. Every day, my man Randy and I would drive all the way into East New York in Brooklyn to get our fix.

More and more people who I knew were all starting to mess with dope. I found myself bringing back heroin to practically everyone in town. Randy and I were driving back with almost twenty bundles a day. Shortly after this started, we began taking orders for cocaine also. And just like that, I was dealing again.

This suddenly became a very dangerous ride. If we got caught, we would be looking at serious prison time. Heroin dealers were made examples of when judges got a hold of them. Nelson then brought in a guy to deliver his packages for him. Randy and I would call Nelson and place an order, then he would have this driver meet us somewhere. We usually met at a Burger King on Rockaway Boulevard right off the Belt Parkway.

On one particular evening that was gorgeous with a pink sky that was slowly fading to darkness, I placed an order with Nelson for ten bundles of heroin and a half- ounce of coke. Randy and I were supposed to meet Nelson's driver in the Burger King parking lot. For some odd reason, this fucking jerkoff driver calls us and tells us to wait on the side street next to Burger King instead of the parking lot. I knew this was a stupid idea. So against our best judgment, we did it. The asshole driver left us waiting there for a half hour. What happened next would be a sign of things to come.

Parked on the side street, I cursed out loud. I was growing impatient and started getting an uneasy feeling. Eventually, the delivery guy came around the corner and pulled in front of Randy's Jeep. I jumped into Nelson's car. Just as I handed the driver a wad of cash, a police van rolled up to us. The driver then panicked and threw a baggie stuffed with heroin and cocaine into my lap. The two cops in the van then jumped out and walked up to Nelson's car. Re- acting quickly, I shoved the package into my underwear. Thank God I was wearing bikini briefs and not boxers. The package wedged up between my balls and my asshole. The cops told us to get out of the car, and they began to pat us down. They found nothing. Next they looked through the car, and again came up empty. Thinking it was over, my confidence was short-lived.

Minutes later, two more police vans rolled up and at least a dozen cops jumped out, even the captain. *Oh, hell no,* I thought to myself. As the cops began ripping Nelson's car apart, the captain pulled me aside and patted me down. He explained to me that he was going to take me to the station and find, it so I should just hand it over. I told the captain that at one time I had a drug problem but had quit. I then said that I owed these guys some money and that I was scared that I would be hurt if I didn't pay them. The captain then grabbed around my balls and still couldn't find it. I pulled down my pants a little and shook my ass to show them I had nothing to hide. The package was wedged so perfectly under my sack, the cops couldn't find it. Finally after pleading my case, the captain said, "Get the fuck out of here." I knew the cops found the money, so I had to come up with a plausible explanation as to why the driver had so much money. The cops bought it. God, was that close. Jumping back into Randy's Jeep, we took off and finally exhaled. We were fortunate to have dodged a bullet.

Fright night was far from over, though. Jason and my mother's boyfriend Steve were eagerly awaiting our arrival back home. They were all smiles when they saw us pull up in front of my father's house. Randy and I got out of his truck and they followed us into my basement apartment. By now I was speed balling, so I promptly threw three bags of heroin and a dime of coke into the spoon and cooked it up. After fixing up, I briefed Steve and Jason on our near catastrophic incident. A call came on my phone, and I decided to take it outside for some privacy. I was on the phone about ten minutes, but while I was outside, Randy asked Jason to shoot him up. He had never done it before; he only snorted dope. By the time I got off the phone, Jason had injected Randy with a bag and a half of the smack that was really strong.

When I reentered the apartment, Jason told me that he had just fixed Randy up. In a slightly relaxed posture, Randy sat back and said, "Holy shit is this good." None of us really paid too much attention to Randy for the next few moments.

Only five minutes later I looked over and noticed Randy on his back. I said, "Are you okay?" There was no response. When I went over to him, I noticed his lips were blue, and his complexion was a dull gray. Oh God, no. Instantly, I screamed for Jason and Steve to help me. Randy wasn't breathing anymore. I started performing CPR while Jason called 911. As I was busy doing CPR, Steve put all the drugs and needles in a bag, ran them down my backyard, and tossed it over the fence into my neighbor's yard. The three of us then carried Randy outside and gently laid him down on the patio. Seven minutes later, my yard was crawling with cops and paramedics.

The paramedics immediately noticed the puncture mark on Randy's arm. They knew what it was and asked me if he shot heroin. I replied by saying, "I think he did, but he didn't do it here." Swiftly, the paramedics hit Randy with some Narcan. In seconds, my buddy was wide awake. Thank God. I was ecstatic to see Randy alive and well. Thanks to my quick thinking, Randy's life was saved.

That was only the beginning. The cops rounded up Steve, Jason, and I and then separated us. They began questioning us about what went down. All three of us played dumb and gave the same answer, which was, "I didn't see anything." My father heard the commotion from his room and was just in disbelief at what was going on when he popped his head out the window. In the yard was Randy on a stretcher with paramedics attending to him, and about ten cops hassling Steve, Jason, and I. What a fucking scene it was. Every neighbor in a four block radius was on my street, wondering what happened. The two ambulances and nine cop cars only made things look that much worse.

Soon after Randy was taken away by ambulance, the cops decided to just go into my apartment and start looking around. I asked them where their warrant was. They told me to shut the fuck up and not move. "Yeah, yeah whatever," I replied. After they meticulously ransacked my crib, they came up with nothing.

When the cops were leaving, and let's just say they were beyond angry they said, "We will see you again."

"Thanks for violating my civil rights," I yelled back at them. Things calmed down soon after they were gone. What do you think I did as soon as the cops left? That's right, I went into my neighbor's yard, grabbed the rest of my shit, and got high. Between nearly getting busted in Queens early that night and my man Randy almost dying, we were walking a razor's edge.

Following the recent misadventure, things just got crazier and crazier. It was hard to fathom that only a couple of years earlier, I was in complete control of my life. Now I was at the opposite end of the spectrum. I was in free fall and totally out of control. My mother stopped by to see me one night, and when I walked out to her car, she nearly had a stroke after looking at me. Her eyes closed for a second, and then a flood of tears rolled down her face. I had lost nearly twenty pounds of muscle, and my eyes looked like two piss holes in the snow. With all this running and gunning, I never really stopped and looked at myself in the mirror. All of a sudden, I caught a glimpse of my reflection in my mom's car window. Good God, I resembled one of those zombies from Night of the Living Dead. It was hard to look my mother in the eye; I was so ashamed. My mother's hazel eyes then gazed at my arms. She became even more upset when she saw the track marks covering my arms. I confessed to her that I was in a bad way and let her know I would try to get help. It was a half-hearted response to calm her down. I was in way too deep, so it would be hard to voluntarily stop.

Now well into 2001, things were about to come full circle for some of us. My old buddy Jake Armstrong, who had lived the last ten years on the lam as a fugitive, was about to get a harsh dose of reality. He was now living in his parents' condo in Georgia and settled into somewhat of a routine life as a father and a family man. You can't outrun karma though, especially when you have been as naughty as Jake had been years earlier back in New York. One night while he was home watching TV, he looked out his window and saw all kinds of federal agents approaching his pad. He knew he was caught. The Feds surrounded the whole complex, so there was nowhere to go. After ten years of avoiding the law, it was now over. They cuffed him, stuffed him, and took him to some detention center. Within a month, Jake was extradited and transported to the county jail in Riverhead, New York. I hadn't seen him in about five years and was unaware that we were about to have a reunion behind bars.

Between bad investments, nonstop spending, and my insatiable desire for heroin, I was nearly broke. Over the years, I made a shitload of money and now had little to show for it. Being in this position, I started working again. I continued to teach karate and even took a bouncing job at some strip club in Huntington. As strung out as I was, I had a lot of trouble keeping up with my responsibilities. While working at the club, I would be nodding off while sitting on my stool at the door checking IDs. I lost the job within a few months. The point of a needle was running my life. How good or bad I felt depended upon when or how much I could inject. My physiological state would slowly start to deteriorate. My psyche became fractured like a jigsaw puzzle. I did however get another job right away. The job was once again a bouncing gig. My buddy Sean McGuire got it for me, and it was at the popular China Club in Manhattan, where all the celebrities frequented.

This one night before work, while I was driving through Wyandanch, I was pulled over. I had two small bags of cocaine on me and one bag of heroin that I forgot about in my wallet. The cops never found the cocaine, but they did find the bag of heroin that was in my wallet. I was arrested on the spot. That one lousy bag was about to cause me more aggravation than I bargained for. For over a decade, I had sold millions and millions of dollars' worth of drugs and never got caught. Now being the junkie that I was, I became so careless and sloppy that I got pinched with a freaking dime bag. It got me a date in drug court in Central Islip.

Going back and forth every three or four weeks to drug court was a pain in the ass. How the hell could I have been so damn foolish? Well, that didn't matter now, so I hired one of my childhood friends named Ted, who was a lawyer. Ted was able to get a few adjournments in the beginning, but on one of those court dates, the judge demanded urine from me. What? I hadn't been convicted yet, so I thought this was total bullshit. The judge then says, "If you don't take the urine test, I'm locking you up." My urine was filthy dirty with heroin and cocaine. I agreed to take the test. After peeing in a cup and testing positive, I said, "Fuck it," and never returned to the courtroom. I absconded from drug court, and a warrant was issued for my arrest.

My friend and lawyer Ted now had a bit of a paradox on his hands. On one hand, he was my lawyer whose job was to keep me out of jail. And on the other hand, he was my friend. And after seeing the condition I was in in court, he was contemplating turning me in to the warrant squad because he was worried I would die if I kept shooting up. Lucky for him, he didn't have to make the call. The warrant squad picked me up a few days later. When I was put back in front of the same judge I absconded from in court, he raised my bail to $50,000. I wasn't going anywhere. My next stop was going to be the county jail in Riverhead where I would be forced to detox.

By the time I got to county lockup, I was already in the early stages of withdrawal. The stench coming from my body was appalling. I was yawning constantly, and my eyes were watery. You could literally smell the heroin coming out of my pores. It was God awful. While going through processing, they sent me to the medial facility. When I walked in, who do you think I saw? My old pal and dealing partner Jake. He was sitting down to see the doctor. He had been cooling his heels now for months, waiting to go to trial for his prior sins he committed before becoming a fugitive. Jake broke the cardinal rule when living on the lamb, complacency. No matter how tempting, you can never keep in contact with people back home because eventually someone is going to turn your ass in. That's what happened to him. Now his fate laid in the hands of some pissed off District Attorney and a hanging judge.

Jake's face was one of surprise when I walked into the room. We gave each other a big hug and for a few minutes, we almost forgot we were in jail. "Man, you are ripe," was the first thing he said to me.

"I'm kicking hard, buddy," I responded. We talked for a good half hour and I brought him up to speed on all current goings on in Huntington. An hour later, we were in different sections of the jail. That would be the last time Jake and I would see each other for the next thirteen years. It was amazing in this lifestyle that you could be here one moment and then gone forever. Jake was eventually sentenced to five to fifteen years in prison.

Kicking dope in jail was a dreadful experience that I wouldn't wish on my worst enemy. Trying to detox in the comfort of your own home is bad enough, but doing it cold turkey in a 6 by 8 cell on 23 hour lockdown is enough to drive anyone insane.

When the sadistic guard on my tier locked my cell door, the agony was just beginning. The scumbag CO really reveled in my discomfort. Gradually, the symptoms of my withdrawal increased in intensity, somewhat like a wave that starts out small only to build to this massive wave until it splashes ashore and in finally gone. As I lay there staring at the dirty gray walls, watching mice run in and out of my cell, I tried to think of anything other than my suffering. It didn't work for long. Within a few hours, I was puking my brains out and had explosive diarrhea. Soon after that, my blood began to feel like it was boiling, while at the same time my skin had goose flesh and was freezing on the outside. It is truly a strange phenomena. Time moves really slowly in jail. Seconds feel like minutes. Minutes like hours, and hours like days. Any sleep I got was filled with night terrors and demonic imagery. I dreamt I was desperately trying to climb the walls while being chased by ghouls and goblins. The dreams were bad enough to make you think you were indeed losing your mind. Your hearing became amplified so even the slightest whisper sounded like a madman was howling in your ear. It took over a week for me to only feel slightly better. I only stayed in jail for three weeks, but it felt like three months. I was humbled for the moment, but not enough to stay clean. When I got home, the first thing I did was reward myself by fixing up with some China white. After all that torture of getting clean, the misery cycle started all over again. That in itself shows you just how fucked up addiction is.

The morning of September 11, 2001, was quite picturesque. The sun was warm, and there were few clouds in the sky. My father and I were making deliveries for his Oscar Meyer route and were stuck in traffic on 495. Listening to Howard Stern, we weren't sure when he reported that a plane had hit the World Trade Center if it was true. Only minutes later we could see the dark smoke rising over lower Manhattan. My father, who was a New York City firefighter for 31 years, couldn't stop staring at the scene. He looked over at me and said, "A lot of people are going to die today."

He couldn't have been more right. We had a van full of meat that had to be delivered to the Bronx before it spoiled. So my dad put the pedal to the floor, and we raced uptown to drop the stuff off. In the time it took us to get to the Bronx, another plane hit the tower of the trade center. Both skyscrapers would tumble to the ground a short time later. There were over 3,000 people killed. By the time we were finished delivering, the police started closing all the bridges and roadways down due to the uncertainty of the situation. There was pandemonium everywhere. My dad and I were lucky because we were able to get over the Throg's Neck Bridge right before they shut it down. My heart ached for the victims of this historic tragedy, but I had my own problems, as did thousands of other junkies in New York. With such a massive security presence and people not allowed on any of the highways or trains, a drug panic set in all over the tri-state area.

That night, as most of the people across the country were glued to their TV sets, dopers and other creepy crawlers were hell bent on finding a way into the city to get their fix, and that included myself. I asked Randy to drive into Brooklyn and cop for us because we were both dry. Randy came through huge and did it. He took back roads all the way into Brooklyn and back. When he returned, I gave him a big hug. The crazy thing was you would have thought we would have been thinking about the attacks and everything that happened that day, but that took a back seat to us scoring our dope.

The handwriting was on the wall. I was heading for an early grave if I didn't pump the brakes and put a halt to what I was doing. My life was basically circling the drain day by day, and I could feel the grim reaper hovering around me. As bad as it was getting, I still could not find the will to pull it together and take back control of my life. Getting high was no longer fun for me at all. I was only trying to stave away the sickness. That was sad considering I was shooting anywhere from ten to fifty bags a day, depending upon what kind of money I had.

Dealing heroin was now the way I was able to keep my habit going. It was really stupid, though. The cops never forgot about the overdose at my apartment, and they kept an ever-watchful eye on my movements. My hookup Nelson got pinched, so I got myself a new supplier named C-Lo, who lived on Knickerbocker Avenue in Bushwick, Brooklyn. Copping dope on Knickerbocker was an extremely risky endeavor. The area was flaming hot with cops all over the place. In a torrential downpour one evening when I entered the four-story building to cop, I didn't notice the building was under surveillance. Once I reached the fourth floor, C-Lo was waiting there with my twenty bundles. Just as we made the exchange of cash and drugs, the door to the building came flying open. In rushed a dozen cops. C-Lo told me to follow him and we both bolted for the roof. We could hear the pitter patter of their feet scurrying up the stairs, so C-Lo and I started jumping from one building to another in the dark. The drop between buildings was over forty feet. We ended up three buildings over and went in a door that led to a staircase. C-Lo and I hurried down the stairs and ended up coming out on an adjacent street to Knickerbocker called Jefferson Avenue. Panting hard, I cautiously weaved my way up the block and made it back to my Jeep and left. Yet, another really close call. How many more of these close encounters could I survive? The answer was not many. If I was a cat, I burned through at least seven lives by now.

Somewhere along the line, I started taking all the wrong turns. It was never more evident than right now. Someone looking from the outside in would see I had become the lowest form of scumbag on the totem pole. A bottom-feeder. I was downright pathetic.

Over the next several months, the police make repeated attempts to knock me off my perch. As usual, they were unsuccessful. They were so frustrated they even resorted to parking police cars at both ends of my blocks during peak business hours of mine. They pulled over anyone who even slowed down near my house. It was more a nuisance than anything else. I couldn't blame them for trying because there was another overdose at my house when someone again almost died. Something had to eventually give.

One afternoon, I walked out in front of my house and saw about ten plain-clothes cops on my driveway, ripping my Jeep apart. They had a friend of mine handcuffed and laying on my driveway with his pants pulled down. My eyes could not believe what they were seeing. Once the cops noticed me, three of them grabbed me by the neck and threw me up against my garage door. Laughing at them, I asked where their warrant was. "You are a cocky little fuck," yelled one of the cops. They began choking me. Another officer pulled out his gun and swung it at my face. He missed.

My neighbor next door, Mr. LaRocca, stepped on to his porch and asked if I was okay. "Get their badge numbers," I asked Mr. LaRocca as my lip began swelling.

The cop who was choking me whispered in my ear, "We are going to set you up and put you away for life whether we find something on you or not. And if we can't, we will just kill you." The scariest part about the threat is he was dead serious. After telling my mother what happened, she begged me to move. She even offered to pay for my relocation. Without any delay, I packed my bags and left that night. Until I reached my destination, there would be "No sleep til….Brooklyn."

Never in a million years would I have believed I would be broke and living in the East New York section of Brooklyn, but that is where I found myself. The reason I chose to settle down there was that was where the dope was. My first week was spent bouncing around and living on the street like some nomad. Thank Goodness my mom stepped in and put me up at a hotel. Every day my focus was on one thing, getting high. Living in Brooklyn as a doper was like letting a kid loose in a candy store. Drugs could be bought literally on almost any block. But my money was now scarce, so I started spending more and more time in withdrawal and dope sick. It really began wearing me out.

There was one major problem with me now living in that area, and that was I stuck out like a turd in a punch bowl. East New York was predominantly a black and Hispanic neighborhood. It shouldn't have, but this would cause all types of problems, big problems. Not with the people there, with the police. The police in the hood were totally different than on Long Island. I called them concrete cowboys. Flat out they did whatever the fuck they wanted, making the rules up as they went along. The 75th Precinct had long been known as one of the worst houses in the entire city. It wouldn't be long before they rolled out the welcome wagons for me.

Running the streets got old pretty fast. It will burn you out in no time. That is the place I found myself after six or eight months of living in Brooklyn. I yearned for a change, and for the first time in a while, I would make a smart decision. Someone talked me into going on the methadone maintenance program. I started on a program that was on Prospect Place in Crown Heights down the street from St. Mary's Hospital.

Methadone gets a bad rap. It is a synthetic opioid analgesic invented by German scientists in the late 1930s. Following World War II, American scientists started tinkering with using methadone as a replacement narcotic for people who were addicted to heroin. In 1971, the first methadone maintenance clinics were opened here in the United States. The idea behind them was to get addicts to switch from heroin to methadone by starting off on a low dose of methadone, and then gradually increasing it until they reached a dose that would have a blocking effect on the heroin. Once that happens, the patient can stabilize their life a little bit at a time. Some people think methadone is a cop out and only gets the addict to switch drugs, but there is a lot more to it than that. It really can work if you work the program correctly.

The final two months prior to joining the methadone program were severely painful. I was running on fumes. Living fix to fix was a punishing existence, and I could no longer keep it up. The toll all the drug use had on my appearance was plain as day. My complexion fluctuated between a funeral-parlor gray to a flushed red when I was high. I had lost nearly forty pounds and almost looked emaciated. Both my arms and legs were covered in track marks, bruises, and open sores that were bleeding. During one brief stay in a detox, the hospital did some blood work on me and the results were terrifying. The doctor told me my T-cell count was 12. A T-cell count that low usually indicated that you have AIDS. It scared the living daylights out of me. After taking multiple HIV tests, it showed I wasn't HIV positive. Praise the Lord. But it did tell the doctors I was partying myself to death. That is why I joined the meth program. There really wasn't much of a choice. I had gotten to the point where I was stealing and even prostituting myself to gay men in order to get my fix.

Entering the clinic on Prospect Place, I wasn't prepared for what I was about to see. After rounding the corner once inside, I found myself in a large room filled with a bunch of people who looked as tore up as anyone I had ever seen. A lot of them looked worse than me, and I looked horrendous. It was like a carnival of oddities. Most of the people in there were HIV positive, had no teeth, and moved with the fluidity of a zombie. Three quarters of the patients were sporting canes or wheelchairs. This was a world most people didn't even know existed.

While waiting impatiently on line, it was finally my time to get my dose. Downing it quickly, I followed a few of the people up the block to a McDonald's on Eastern Parkway where all the fellow methadonians would congregate and await their buzz to kick in. Looking around, I thought to myself, *My how the mighty have fallen.* It was just incomprehensible that I was where I was. I went from running a million dollar drug business to being a sickly junkie. The reality was I was just as sick with this disease as all the other people. Following a hot cup of coffee, a strong buzz hit my system, and I began mingling with some of the others on the program. As sad as it was, this would be my routine for the next few years.

Brooklyn had a well-deserved reputation for being one of the violent places in the country. I would start to witness a lot of it up close and personal. One morning after getting my daily dose of methadone, I stepped outside of the program and started talking to a few people. While I was standing there, I saw this guy Skip swing a box cutter at another guy's face. Immediately, this man screamed and grabbed his jaw. You could see blood spurting all over the place. When he pulled his hand away, there was an eight-inch gash from his ear to his chin as thick as a rope. Skip thought this guy had picked up a $5 bill he had dropped. His punishment was getting sliced with a box cutter that could have killed him. Over $5, man people in the hood did not fuck around. Shit like this went on all the time where I was now living.

That same day only a few hours later, I was walking back to my hotel when I decided to duck into this fast food joint on Pennsylvania Avenue and fix up. I scored a few bags of dope at the program. When I tried going into the bathroom, I noticed it was locked. I knocked and no one answered. Upon waiting a few minutes, I decided to ask the manager to open the restroom. The manager pounded on the door, and still there was no answer. "This can't be good," said the manager. The manager took a key and unlocked the door. There on the toilet was some junkie, with a needle in his arm, who appeared to be dead. My stomach felt sick after seeing that, so I split. I couldn't get that image from my mind for a long time.

November 2004 was wicked cold, and the winds that were howling chilled you to the bone. Once again, I wound up on the street with nowhere to stay. My dear mother was financially tapped out and needed a break from carrying my hobo ass. I got lucky, and ended up crashing at some lady's crib I met on the program. Her name was Carmen, and she really did me a solid. Carmen left me alone in her apartment for a few days when she had to go away to visit her family. One of those nights she was gone, I accidentally got locked out of the building. It was located on Lafayette Avenue in the Bedford Stuyvesant section of Brooklyn.

Now freezing my ass off, I ended up knocking on the window of some downstairs apartment where some old woman lived. I was delighted when the door opened. Standing inside was this stunningly beautiful black woman. She cracked this incredible smile and said, "Come in." My heart skipped a beat as I stepped in out of the cold. She then asked me if I wanted to come into the old woman's apartment that she was visiting. I said, "Sure." We introduced ourselves and she told me her name was Christine. I said, "I'm Patrick." Talk about love at first sight. I got this weird feeling in my chest as we struck up a conversation. It had been ages since I had felt like that. The old woman was giggling her ass off after noticing Christine and I had a mutual attraction for one another. I wasted no time in asking Christine if she wanted to have lunch with me. She said yes. I was elated once it sank in as to what was happening.

That Thursday, we met at the house where I was staying. We walked down the street to a small café on Broadway by the J train. Christine looked absolutely radiant. Her complexion was a flawless medium brown, and her almond shaped eyes were dark and mysterious. She had a body that was voluptuous. During our lunch, Christine told me a lot about herself. She grew up only blocks away, on Putnam Avenue. We had a wonderful time together, and I enjoyed myself so much I surprisingly forgot all about my own problems that had been plaguing me for a long time. It was just what the doctor ordered. After finishing lunch, we took a long walk to this park where we sat on a bench and continued talking. I looked deep into her eyes and laid a passionate kiss on her soft lips. Bells went off immediately. It was as if there was some cosmic explosion in my brain. That one date would blossom into quite a romantic relationship. And meeting Christine ended up as a jumping off point to repairing my broken life. She was a Godsend.

Shortly after our relationship began, I had to move again. There was a room available in a three-story house in East New York, on Nicholls Avenue. My mom helped me to get in there fairly quickly. By now, thanks to Christine, I totally stopped using heroin. The fog was slowly starting to lift around me, and things began improving. That was until one fateful day where I was in the wrong place at the wrong time.

Minding my own business, I began strutting down Fulton Street making my way to the J train. I was going to head over to Christine's father's house to see if she was there. The afternoon was somewhat dreary, with dark clouds and a damp coolness in the air. An ominous feeing started to wash over me. In the past, that usually meant something wasn't right. My senses were right on. Lurking in the distance were some over-zealous police officers from Brooklyn North Narcotics, ready to try to meet some unwritten quota in which they try to arrest a certain amount of people each day. Lucky me, this would be my lucky day.

Stop and frisk, in reality, should be called stop, harass, and make up some reason to arrest someone who is minding his own business. That is the way Johnny Law does it in the hood. It's an absolute fucking disgrace. When I got to the corner of Crescent and Fulton, I stopped for the light. When crossing the street, I saw my neighbor Felix, who was standing on the corner with a few of his pals. I said to Felix, "What up, yo?" and he gave me a fist bump. The cops who were watching that spot assumed we did a hand to hand. They were wrong!

Public Enemy's song, "Welcome to the Terror Dome" had just started playing on my headphones when I left Felix and began to walk toward the subway stop only twenty yards away. Right as I reached the stairs to enter the subway, something made me turn around. I saw some white guy in regular clothes running my way. He was about 50 years old. I turned back the other way to see who he was running after. No one was there. As soon as I turned back again, this white guy grabbed me by my shirt. Pulling off my headphones, I grabbed the guy by his shirt and said, "What the fuck is your problem?" It turned out that he was a cop from Brooklyn North Narcotics, and he never identified himself. It was on right there.

In seconds and without provocation, another five or six cops pounced on me. They came out of nowhere. It was now six on one. A wild brawl was now underway right on the sidewalk, and a huge crowd now gathered around to witness it. While the one cop and I were tangled up in a wrestling match, the other five cops started kicking and punching me like a bunch of savages. I refused to go down and it pissed them off the more I resisted. This went on for a good two minutes. I finally went down, on my stomach to let them put the cuffs on me. But before they cuffed me, one of the officers jumped on my back and pulled out his radio and started bashing my head in with it. He hit me at least twenty times and didn't stop until he cracked my head open. The others continued kicking me in my ribs and face. My head was bleeding profusely, and a huge pool of blood appeared on the sidewalk. It's like the police were in a state of blood lust. They weren't satisfied until they felt like they had made their point, which was beating me into submission. The crowd grew restless and demanded that the cops stop hitting me. Their guns were now drawn, and they were looking to shoot somebody. The ordeal finally ended.

A few moments later, an ambulance arrived and hauled me off to Jamaica Hospital. I had two black eyes, bruises up and down my entire body, and a head wound that needed attention. It ended up taking a dozen metal staples to close my head back up. Those mother fucking bastards. I was so fucking pissed off. After leaving the hospital, I was taken to the 75th Precinct on Sutter Avenue for booking. When I was locked up in a cell, one of the cops came over and asked me if I was on angel dust. "Hell no," I replied. He said they had never had that much trouble taking someone down. My stay at the 75th Precinct was about six hours.

The next stop on this lovely tour was central booking on Schermerhorn Street in downtown Brooklyn for arraignment. Central booking is a total shit hole. It is basically a labyrinth of holding cells one after another that is on every floor as you make your way up the building to the courtrooms. The cells were filthy and overcrowded with criminals who were herded through like cattle, all awaiting their fate to be decided by some judge. Going through the system is what they call, "Bullpen Therapy," and in the city you can wait as long as three days to see the judge. When I was tossed into the cage, I got mad respect from all the other criminals for fighting with the police. I was also informed that I could sue the city for what the cops did to me. Hey, a silver lining.

Well it took me nearly three days to get in front of the judge. I was being charged with three felony counts of assault on a police officer with intent to bodily harm and a slew of lesser charges. I figured my bail would be a half million dollars, but it wasn't. Some black judge who I was fortunate to be in front of took one look at me and said, ROR, released on my own recognizance. Damn, was I happy. I hired a lawyer and he sued the City of New York, and I did get some money. This only made the bullseye on my back that much bigger because some of the cops did get into trouble.

It took months to get over the shock of what happened with the police. I kind of fell back into a mundane life of going back and forth to the program and not doing much else with my life. Occasionally, I took some odd jobs to try to keep my head above water. For a while, I had some of my students who I taught karate come all the way into Brooklyn for lessons. The only real satisfying thing in my life was spending time with Christine, my woman. And it was awesome. It overshadowed all of the other things that weren't so great at that time. The house I lived in started falling apart, and for some reason the landlord abandoned the place. The heat was turned off along with the hot water. We also had terrible problems with rats and roaches. There was a guy living next door to me who was selling crack cocaine. That became a gigantic problem because crack heads started hanging around the house, which brought all kinds of headaches with law enforcement. The cops raided the house on multiple occasions, thanks to my neighbor, and dragged me in with him even though I had nothing to do with it. It was total horseshit. In all, I would be locked up another six or seven times, thanks to the vindictive police looking for some payback from when I sued them. It was more harassment than anything else, but I did end up making multiple stops at C-95 in Riker's Island. Before I knew it, years had gone by.

I had seen enough, though. This life had completely done me in. Little by little, I began to change my life. It was time. Life in the fast lane was simply too much for me. After a long struggle with addiction and being a criminal, the time was right for unconditional surrender. In 2008, I finally began detoxing off the methadone. That took quite some time, nearly a year, and it practically broke me in the process. It would take years to bounce back from that. With a twelve-step program, a strong belief in God, and the help of Narcotics Anonymous, things started looking up. Christine was the one who really played the biggest factor in the end. Don't ever underestimate what the power of a good woman's love can do. With her help, somehow I managed to summon enough strength to take back possession of my soul.

On an ordinary morning in 2008, I walked up to the corner store to get some coffee and the newspaper. When I looked at the front page of one of the New York papers, I was flabbergasted. There on the cover was my old buddy Chris Campanella of the Crash and Carry Gang, being led away in handcuffs by two FBI agents. The caption read, "Businessman Arrested in Three Cold Case Murders." After reading the article, I sat on the curb and just shook my head. The story went something like this:

It all started back in 1994, when the armed robbery of an armored car ended in disaster. I mentioned it earlier in the book. One of the guards was shot and killed during the robbery. According to law enforcement, Chris Campanella and a few of his crew were the ones who did it. They got away initially and burned the get-away vehicle. Months later, the body of one of the accomplices was found floating in a tool chest about ten miles off the coast of Long Island. He had been murdered. Then around 2001, some guy who was a longtime friend of Chris' was shot and killed in broad daylight on a street in Manhattan. The Feds did their due diligence connecting all three murders, but still didn't have enough to bring Chris in. Sometime in 2008, the FBI caught a break. In 1994, science couldn't do enough to prove who had done it. When CSI originally processed the burnt get away vehicle, they found a few hairs, but DNA was in its infancy so it couldn't link Chris to the robbery yet. By 2008, scientific technology had advanced enough to get a DNA hit from the hairs that were found in the burnt up SUV. The Feds got their arrest warrant and picked up Chris Campanella.

In 2012, Chris went on trial for all three murders. The District Attorney painted a picture of a career criminal, who after the armored car heist decided to eliminate any remaining witnesses who could connect him to the crime. By the time the Feds picked Chris up, he had parlayed the money from all the robberies into becoming a successful businessman. Some people were shocked when all this came out, but not me. Even though I was a friend of Chris', I knew he could be ruthless. After the DA got Chris' longtime friend Scott O'-Connor to roll on Chris and testify in court, it was a done deal. Chris Campanella was convicted of all three murders and is now serving three life sentences in federal prison. It's this whole damn criminal lifestyle; it brings out the worst in everyone.

My former partner in crime, Big Ray Scalzo, made a few million dollars hustling cocaine and robbing people after we put the kibosh on our arch nemesis Ira Kilstein in 1992. By 1996, Big Ray made off with all his cash and split the Huntington scene all together. He reemerged in 2008 after laying low nearly a decade. Around this time, he became fully entrenched in the exploding marijuana trade in northern California and made a fortune in a short time. Right before he got out of business, a guy from Huntington was robbed and murdered up in Sonoma County north of San Francisco. Big Ray had nothing to do with it, but it looked awfully coincidental. The cops eventually nailed the killers, and they all got life sentences. After that, Twinkie slipped away like a phantom in the middle of the night and reappeared back in New York. Knowing Big Ray as well as I do, I have no doubt that criminal bastard is up to no good wherever he is.

In 2000, one of my old weed connects, Charlie Sykes, was kidnapped and held for ransom in Tucson, Arizona, by the Mexican mob for the $585,000 he owed them for the load that got busted back in 1990. He had to be rescued by a federal SWAT team and his whereabouts are unknown at this time.

My original training and dealing partner, Jake Armstrong, was released from prison in 2006 after doing five years, and he went on the straight and narrow. He remarried in 2012 not long after his first wife Tina died of a drug overdose that same year.

Vanessa, my kid's mother, could not stop getting high. She ended up doing three state bids, the last one a three-year stretch for bank robbery. As of now, she was home and attempting to rebuild her life. I wish her nothing but the best.

And as for me, I left Brooklyn in 2010 and moved back to Long Island, a truly humbled man. I made it through the darkest time in my life and was now drug free and back in my daughter's life. We as human beings are resilient and have the ability to outshine the world's greatest darkness. As long as we believe in ourselves, we can overcome anything. Looking back, I can honestly say that what my buddies and I were involved with was wrong. We were wrong. Every one of us took shortcuts for the lure of fast money and wound up broke or in jail. Karma had the last laugh in the end. Although none of us were in business any more, there were plenty of newcomers that would fill the void left by our departure. And believe it or not, these new hustlers would be just dumb enough to think they were smart enough to get away with something very few ultimately ever do. Their prison cells are awaiting them. But make no mistake about it; we are losing the war on drugs. We are in danger of losing an entire generation to opiate addiction and other drugs that are being abused. It's going to take a monumental effort to come up with a solution. The clock is ticking. So let this be a cautionary tale to anyone who is thinking about embarking on a life of crime or being involved with narcotics. There is no riding off into the sunset, no Hollywood endings when it comes to drugs and crime. You will be lucky to escape with your freedom, and most importantly, your life!

The End.

Epilogue

After reading this book, it begs the question as to what caused this generation to go so far off the reservation. The peace, free love and LSD taking hippies of the 1960's counterculture gave way to a new generation who would grab the baton and turn up the volume, taking drug use to an extremely reckless and dangerous level. Why did so many kids that had the opportunity to attend good schools and had fairly decent upbringings choose such a self destructive path and willingly throw their lives away for the sake of getting high or chasing a fast buck. Was it the breakdown of the family structure as a society caused by a huge generation gap. It certainly is one contributing factor. Whatever the reason, they need to get ahead of this for the safety and security of the coming generations.

In 2015 there were over 50,000 deaths from drug overdoses in the U.S. In 2016, that number exceeded 60,000.Until the powers that be make this a top priority, it will continue to rise. If they don't, then they better start building more cemeteries, cause there aren't enough vacancies to handle all the new soon to be residents on their way.

Statistics don't lie, but unfortunately, they are trending in the wrong direction. Drugs have been tearing apart the moral fabric of our society for too long. Forget terrorism, narcotics are a greater danger to our population than any outside people will ever be. As I sit tonight writing this, some unfortunate parent will find out the crushing news that their child has succumbed to drug addiction. And they won't be the only ones. This tragedy will repeat itself every single day as time moves forward. There needs to be a better understanding of the situation as a whole in order to address the problem. Education can play a huge factor. The answer is out there somewhere. I did not write this book to give anyone a romantic notion of what being a criminal or a drug user is like. I wanted to reveal the harsh realities that are the consequences that come with the bad choices we make.

"Two roads diverged in a wood. And I, I took the one less travelled by, and that has made all the difference."

—Robert Frost